B

YUI
Yui's STATS

Lv24
HP 35/35
MP 20/20
[STR 325]
[VIT 0]
[AGI 0]
[DEX 0]
[INT 0]

MAI
Mai's STATS

Lv24
HP 35/35
MP 20/20
[STR 325]
[VIT 0]
[AGI 0]
[DEX 0]
[INT 0]

Welcome to
NewWorld Online.

Flames arced through the sky—like
a meteor hurtling toward them.

A girl with white wings and black
armor stood before them.

"HOLY CONDEMNATION!"

The combined might of his allies focused on his glowing blade. Pain swung—!

Bofuri
★ I Don't ★
Want to Get
Hurt, so I'll
④ Max Out My
Defense.

YUUMIKAN

Illustration by **KOIN**

YEN ON
NEW YORK

Welcome to
NewWorld Online.

YUUMIKAN

Translation by Andrew Cunningham ● Cover art by KOIN

ITAINO WA IYA NANODE BOGYORYOKU NI KYOKUFURI SHITAITO OMOIMASU. Vol. 4
©Yuumikan, Koin 2018
First published in Japan in 2018 by KADOKAWA CORPORATION, Tokyo.
English translation rights arranged with KADOKAWA CORPORATION, Tokyo, through TUTTLE-MORI AGENCY, INC., Tokyo.

English translation © 2022 by Yen Press, LLC

Yen On
150 West 30th Street, 19th Floor
New York, NY 10001

Visit us at yenpress.com ● facebook.com/yenpress ● twitter.com/yenpress
yenpress.tumblr.com ● instagram.com/yenpress

First Yen On Edition: January 2022

Yen On is an imprint of Yen Press, LLC.
The Yen On name and logo are trademarks of Yen Press, LLC.

Library of Congress Cataloging-in-Publication Data
Names: Yuumikan, author. I Koin, illustrator. I Cunningham, Andrew, 1979– translator.
Title: Bofuri, I don't want to get hurt, so I'll max out my defense / Yuumikan ; illustration by Koin ; translated by Andrew Cunningham.
Other titles: Itai no wa Iya nano de bōgyoryoku ni kyokufuri shitai to omoimasu. English
Description: First Yen On edition. I New York : Yen On, 2021–
Identifiers: LCCN 2020055872 I ISBN 9781975322731 (v. 1 ; trade paperback) I
    ISBN 9781975323547 (v. 2 ; trade paperback) I ISBN 9781975323561 (v. 3 ; trade paperback) I
    ISBN 9781975323585 (v. 4 ; trade paperback)
Subjects: LCSH: Video gamers—Fiction. I Virtual reality—Fiction. I GSAFD: Science fiction.
Classification: LCC PL874.I46 I8313 2021 I DDC 895.63/6—dc23
LC record available at https://lccn.loc.gov/2020055872

ISBNs: 978-1-9753-2358-5 (paperback)
        978-1-9753-2359-2 (ebook)

10 9 8 7 6 5 4 3 2 1

LSC-C

Printed in the United States of America

CONTENTS

I Don't Want to Get Hurt,
so I'll Max Out My Defense.

NewWorld Online Status

NAME Maple ‖ Maple **LV 35**

HP 200/200 **MP** 22/22

STATUS

STR 000 **VIT** 1235 **AGI** 000 **DEX** 000 **INT** 000

EQUIPMENT

‖ New Moon: Hydra ‖ Night's Facsimile: Devour ‖ Bonding Bridge

‖ Black Rose Armor: Saturating Chaos ‖ Toughness Ring ‖ Life Ring

SKILL

Shield Attack　Sidestep　Deflect　Meditation　Taunt　Inspire　HP Boost (S)　MP Boost (S)

Great Shield Mastery V　Cover Move IV　Cover　Pierce Guard　Counter　Absolute Defense

Moral Turpitude　Giant Killing　Hydra Eater　Bomb Eater　Sheep Eater　Indomitable Guardian

Psychokinesis　Fortress　Martyr's Devotion　Machine God

NewWorld Online Status

NAME Sally ‖ Sally **LV 30**

HP 32/32 **MP** 80/80

STATUS

STR 070 **VIT** 000 **AGI** 158 **DEX** 045 **INT** 050

EQUIPMENT

‖ Deep Sea Dagger ‖ Seabed Dagger

‖ Surface Scarf: Mirage ‖ Oceanic Coat: Oceanic

‖ Oceanic Clothes ‖ Black Boots ‖ Bonding Bridge

SKILL

Gale Slash　Defense Break　Inspire　Down Attack　Power Attack　Switch Attack

Combo Blade IV　Martial Arts V　Fire Magic II　Water Magic III　Wind Magic III　Earth Magic II

Dark Magic II　Light Magic II　Strength Boost (S)　Combo Boost (S)　MP Boost (S)　MP Cost Down (S)

MP Recovery Speed Boost (S)　Poison Resist (S)　Gathering Speed Boost (S)　Dagger Mastery V

Magic Mastery III　Affliction III　Presence Block II　Presence Detect II　Sneaky Steps I　Leap III

Cooking I　Fishing　Swimming X　Diving X　Shearing　Superspeed　Ancient Ocean

Chaser Blade　Jack of All Trades　Sword Dance

I Don't Want to Get Hurt, so I'll Max Out My Defense

Welcome to NewWorld Online

NAME Chrome HP 840/840 MP 52/52 LV 56

STATUS

STR 125 VIT 175 AGI 020 DEX 020 INT 010

EQUIPMENT

- Headhunter: Life Eater
- Wrath Wraith Wall: Soul Syphon
- Bloodstained Skull: Soul Eater
- Bloodstained Bone Armor: Dead or Alive
- Robust Ring
- Impregnable Ring
- Defense Ring

SKILL

Thrust   Flame Slash   Ice Blade   Shield Attack   Sidestep   Deflect   Great Defense
Taunt   Impregnable Stance   HP Boost (L)   HP Recovery Speed Boost (L)   MP Boost (S)
Great Shield Mastery X   Defense Mastery X   Cover Move X   Cover   Pierce Guard   Counter
Guard Aura   Poison Resist (L)   Paralyze Resist (M)   Stun Resist (M)   Sleep Resist (M)
Freeze Resist (M)   Burn Resist (S)   Mining IV   Gathering V   Shearing   Spirit Light
Indomitable Guardian   Battle Healing

NAME Iz HP 100/100 MP 100/100 LV 40

STATUS

STR 045 VIT 020 AGI 065 DEX 210 INT 030

EQUIPMENT

- Blacksmith Hammer X
- Alchemist Goggles: Faustian Alchemy
- Alchemist Long Coat: Magic Workshop
- Blacksmith Leggings X
- Alchemist Boots: New Frontier
- Potion Pouch
- Item Pouch
- Black Gloves

SKILL

Strike   Crafting Mastery X   Enhance Success Rate Boost (L)   Gathering Speed Boost (L)
Mining Speed Boost (L)   Affliction II   Sneaky Steps III   Smithing X   Sewing X   Horticulture X
Synthesizing X   Augmentation X   Cooking X   Mining X   Gathering X   Swimming IV   Diving V
Shearing   Godsmith's Grace VIII

NAME Kanade HP 335/335 MP 290/290 LV 22

STATUS

STR 015 VIT 010 AGI 020 DEX 030 INT 110

EQUIPMENT

- Divine Wisdom: Akashic Records
- Diamond Newsboy Cap VIII
- Smart Coat VI
- Smart Leggings VIII
- Smart Boots VI
- Spade Earrings
- Mage Gloves
- Holy Ring

SKILL

Magic Mastery V   MP Boost (M)   MP Cost Down (S)   MP Recovery Speed Boost (M)
Fire Magic III   Water Magic II   Wind Magic III   Earth Magic II   Dark Magic I   Light Magic II
Sorcerer's Stacks

Welcome to NewWorld Online.

NAME **Kasumi** HP 435/435 MP 70/70 LV **54**

STATUS

[STR] 170 [VIT] 080 [AGI] 090 [DEX] 020 [INT] 020

EQUIPMENT

Unsigned Katana	Cherry Blossom Barrette	Cherry Blossom Vestments
Edo Purple Hakama	Samurai Greaves	Samurai Gauntlets
Gold Obi Fastener	Cherry Blossom Crest

SKILL Gleam Helmsplitter Guard Break Sweep Slice Eye for Attack Inspire Sinew Attack Stance Katana Arts X HP Boost (L) MP Boost (S) Poison Resist (L) Paralyze Resist (L) Longsword Mastery X Katana Mastery X Mining IV Gathering VI Diving V Swimming VI Leap VII Shearing Keen Sight Indomitable Sword Spirit Dauntless Superspeed Ever Vigilant

NAME **Mai** HP 35/35 MP 20/20 LV **24**

STATUS

[STR] 325 [VIT] 000 [AGI] 000 [DEX] 000 [INT] 000

EQUIPMENT

| Black Annihilammer VIII | Black Doll Dress VIII | Black Doll Tights VIII |
| Black Doll Shoes VIII | Little Ribbon | Silk Gloves |

SKILL Double Stamp Double Impact Attack Boost (S) Hammer Mastery II Throw Conqueror Annihilator Giant Killing

NAME **Yui** HP 35/35 MP 20/20 LV **24**

STATUS

[STR] 325 [VIT] 000 [AGI] 000 [DEX] 000 [INT] 000

EQUIPMENT

| White Annihilammer VIII | White Doll Dress VIII | White Doll Tights VIII |
| White Doll Shoes VIII | Little Ribbon | Silk Gloves |

SKILL Double Stamp Double Impact Attack Boost (S) Hammer Mastery II Throw Conqueror Annihilator Giant Killing

I Don't Want to Get Hurt, so I'll Max Out My Defense

Welcome to NewWorld Online

Prologue

Maple's extreme defense build had propelled her into the top ranks of players. With her friend Sally, she'd founded the Maple Tree guild. Joining them were the great shielder Chrome, the katana master Kasumi, and a mage named Kanade whose Akashic Records provided him with random skills.

In due time, they added the crafter Iz as well as the twins, Mai and Yui, who had extreme builds. As the fourth event loomed, the guild prepared to face whatever came together. This event would once again speed up the flow of time, pitting guilds against one another as they fought to defend orbs in their bases or steal them from their opponents—vying to earn the most points.

Each death would reduce the player's stats, and a fifth death would eliminate them completely. Maple Tree would have a tough time contending with large guilds that could leverage the power of numbers.

If they wanted to finish at the top, they'd have to strategize.

"Let's aim for the top ten!" Maple cried.

Her friends cheered as they were wreathed in light.

"We've got this!"

As the world went white, Maple clenched her fists tight.

CHAPTER 1

Defense Build and the Fourth Event

As the light faded, the eight members of Maple Tree found themselves before a pedestal. An orb giving off a green glow lay atop it. This location would serve as their base—they would be defending their orb in the depths of a cave.

Much like the second event, the map contained a multitude of biomes. This particular spot was much easier to defend than, say, the middle of a grassy field.

Three paths branched off from the large main cavern.

Sally and Kasumi each investigated one of the paths behind the pedestal. They weren't gone for long.

"This one leads to a dead end with a spring. Good place to rest."

"Mine had nothing of note. I suppose it's a decent place to lie down."

"Then the last path must be the way to the surface. That definitely makes defending easier."

No risk of being attacked from behind.

"Sounds like we'll be on the offense."

"Yep, just like we planned it."

No use wasting time; Sally, Chrome, and Kasumi—the attack squad—swiftly set out from their base.

Sally and Kasumi were the fastest members of the guild, and Chrome could adapt on the fly to any situation. These three would handle the snatch-and-grab missions while Maple held down the fort. Kanade and Iz would be supporting Mai and Yui, who were also playing defense. This event was all about guarding the orbs they stole, so it was important to make sure their base was well defended.

The home team donned the robes Iz provided. She put one on herself and took a seat near the orb. These robes provided no extra defense. They were just cloth, designed to hide everyone's faces. Keeping Maple's presence secret would be critical. Maple Tree's defensive strategy involved convincing people they were a small, weak no-name guild by having Mai and Yui clobber anyone who came after them—with the other three discreetly providing backup as needed.

This would weaken the guilds around them and make things easier for the attack team.

Maple herself was famously dangerous, with a notorious array of insane skills. Any guilds that spotted her were liable to run away.

"If anyone comes in, Mai, Yui, it's your chance to shine! I've got your back!" Maple flourished her shield confidently.

"Okay! I hope we can do this. We did practice a lot..."

"You know we can, Mai! Not...that I don't have butterflies myself..."

They were feeding off each other's anxiety.

"Maple will protect you both," Kanade assured them. "Just focus on attacking and you'll be fine."

"That's right! Leave all defending to me!"

This seemed to help. The twins grinned and pumped their fists.

"Any minute now, the others will start ferrying orbs back here."
They kept a close watch on the entrance, conserving energy and getting ready.

◆□◆□◆□◆□◆

Meanwhile, the attack squad members were moving quietly through the brush deep in a forest.

"We see the enemy, we kill without hesitation—everyone good with that?"

"Fine by me. Let's start by scouting the area around us. We'll eliminate any threats nearby."

Not long after, Sally heard players talking up ahead.

"I'll take point and start thinning their ranks, leading them back to you two; when you see an opening, take it."

"Got it."

"We'll be waiting in this brush."

After they got in position, Sally leaped up into a tree and began bounding from limb to limb, headed toward the voices.

The group they overheard talking contained five people—another guild's attack party, on the prowl for orbs.

"There oughtta be at least one nearby..."

"I'm sure there will be. Stay loose and keep looking."

But just as the last of them passed beneath a tree—

—Sally swung down, her legs hooked over a limb, and sank a dagger into the throat of the one bringing up the rear.

"Aughhhhhhh?!"

Before they could even grasp what was happening, Sally struck again, showing no mercy.

Her victim was still screaming in confusion as their HP hit

zero, and they vanished in a burst of light. The other four spun around, only to get hit by a sharp-edged wind.

The shocking loss of their companion left them badly shaken.

"…………"

Sally was already running away.

"H-hey! Come back here!"

They were so rattled, they made the fatal error of giving chase. Never realizing Sally was leading them straight into a trap.

Just as they thought they'd caught up—

—a katana and a cleaver came whistling out of the underbrush, instantly killing the leader.

"Oh…crap!"

They realized it was a trap—too late.

Kasumi was already cutting down a third foe.

"Retreat…augh!"

One girl turned to run, but Sally's Fire Ball caught her in the back, knocking her off balance.

"Hmph!"

Which left her no way to dodge Chrome's cleaver.

"…Looking good."

"Yup. C'mon."

They'd intentionally let one go.

All alone now, there was no way to challenge another guild. It was obvious the lone survivor would head back to camp. But that player probably should have chosen death instead—

—because *this* was like inviting the devil back home.

Kasumi and Chrome opened their maps, checking Sally's position. There was a red triangle with her name on it, and it was still on the move.

Sally could tail the survivor undetected; they only had to follow the marker on their maps.

"Thataway. Shall we?"

"Yeah. I'll take lead," Chrome said. "Just in case."

They set out, maintaining a safe distance.

"Oh, there you are," Sally called from the tree above.

"Is that the cave?" Kasumi asked.

Sally nodded.

Up ahead was a cave entrance, hidden by the trees—easy to miss.

"Probably a small guild, like us. Maybe just big enough to qualify as midsize. Can't tell how many are in there, exactly."

"Then we stick to the plan. I'll go first. Nothing to worry about."

He had the highest defense and loads of survival skills, so Chrome was their designated base forerunner.

Not far in, he found the orb pedestal.

He also stumbled upon thirty-odd players listening to the survivor's harrowing tale.

All of them were facing the entrance and saw him coming.

"Brace yourselves!" the guild master roared.

Swords were drawn, shields raised, and weapons brandished.

"Here we go." Chrome lunged forward, Sally and Kasumi hot on his heels.

They slammed into the enemy's front line, and Chrome started carving his way in.

He was certainly taking damage—but against this many foes, he was constantly hitting someone and always blocking someone else.

A close examination made it plain to see that the HP bar over his head was refilling completely as soon as it dropped even slightly.

Realizing this, the front-liners tried to back off—and that's when Sally and Kasumi hit them.

The ones in the rear flung a stream of spells, but Sally was slipping through the hail of magic like she could read their minds. And Kasumi was firmly within range of Chrome's Cover.

"You'll have to try harder if you wanna hit me!"

"As elusive a target as ever… If only I could do the same!"

But even as she grumbled, Kasumi was downing foes faster than Sally. While their kill counts were neck and neck, Chrome did his part—and all the more effectively thanks to the girls drawing attention away from him.

The enemy's healing couldn't keep up with their focused assault, and one foe after another disappeared in bursts of scattering light.

"Wh-what do we do?!"

"Their tank's paralyzed! We've gotta take at least *one* out!"

The last-ditch effort paid off, and the status effect took hold— Chrome couldn't move a muscle. Chrome's ability to hold the line depended on his positioning—and the fact that he healed both when attacking and guarding. With those skills out of commission, the damage he was taking outpaced his healing.

"Tch…sure is rough fighting this many!"

Seeing Chrome immobilized, eight players surrounded him and used every skill and spell at their disposal to take him down.

They got close but not close enough.

A red skeleton appeared behind him, and his HP stopped falling—with one point left.

Chrome *should* have died. But when his HP hit zero, his equipment skill, Dead or Alive, gave him a 50 percent chance of surviving with a single point remaining.

And there were no limits. There was a chance the same thing could happen every time he dropped to zero.

"Ha, luck's with me today!"

"Heal!"

Sally's spell topped his health bar up, and the status effect timed out.

As that desperate final attack lost steam, Chrome started hacking into the crowd again, every bit as brutal as before.

"With my old gear, I would've been forced to use Indomitable Guardian. Only Maple could survive being surrounded like that..."

Chrome was a top player himself, but paralyzed, with foes on all sides pounding away? It was a wonder he'd made it out alive. Escaping by the skin of his teeth was the best he could manage.

Kasumi slew the most players. She had the highest DPS in the party and was no slouch in the agility department, either.

As the one party member with heavy armor and a shield, Chrome was an obvious tank, which meant he'd drawn the bulk of attacks and been knocking at death's door. Even so, he wanted to keep his limited use skills in reserve, and taking a few risks was worth it.

The day was only just getting started, and he had already decided which skills *not* to use.

Since he had Indomitable Guardian, he could cheat death once without fail. That was why he'd chosen to not waste any skills that could have helped him avoid death earlier.

"All right, here's the orb. Kasumi, wanna run this home for us? I'm gonna go scout the surroundings. Feels like the guilds might have spawned closer together than I expected."

This event was all about defending and stealing orbs, so Sally retrieved it carefully, making absolutely sure there wasn't someone lying in wait to ambush her.

Leaving her in charge of investigating how densely packed the guilds might be, Chrome and Kasumi escorted their prize back to base. The enemies they'd slain would revive near their base but in random locations, so there was little point trying to camp the respawn points.

While Kasumi and Chrome were heading back home, the other Maple Tree members were fending off an assault.

"Only five defenders! We've got this!"

Eight attackers charged the Maple Tree positions, only to come face-to-face with metal spheres hurled with wild abandon like snowballs. Mai and Yui had given no thought to durability or speed, only raising their STR stat as high as they could—and with Conqueror boosting that even higher, their attack power defied rhyme or reason.

""Hyah!""

Those cute shouts were followed closely by the terrifying *whoosh* of incoming high-speed projectiles.

The enemy tried to take cover behind their shields, but the spheres knocked them *and* their shields down.

They tried to parry some with their blades, but the swords snapped—and the players splattered.

"Here, keep going."

Iz kept placing more spheres at the twins' feet. There was no end in sight.

"...I don't think they *need* my protection."

"Yeah. I'm pretty much useless, too."

Maple and Kanade simply continued to watch the attacking guild suffer under the withering barrage.

The stragglers soon realized this was hopeless and tried to run—but they'd advanced too far, and not a single one made it back to the tunnel entrance. The crunch of a ball connecting with their backs was the last thing they felt.

When the eight players made it back to their base after being battered to death, all they could do was warn the rest of the guild never to go into that cave. That alone was valuable intel.

On her own, Sally was swiftly moving from branch to bush to boulder, constantly staying out of view while she searched for more guilds.

She'd made a wide loop and had already found five. It would still be quite some time before she could grasp the whole event map, but she'd detected a pattern—wherever there were ruins, forests, lakes, or other distinctive landmarks, there was likely a guild nearby.

The five she'd found weren't all small, either. Some were midsize and had as many as fifty-odd players.

Sally made a note of each on her map, then slipped away before anyone saw her.

"Midsize guild, in the ruins—roof over the orb but no walls."

She closed her map and leaned back against the tree trunk, thinking it over.

That last fight had gone just as planned. They'd managed to pull off a win without any losses, but it had been close—and the next one might not go as well.

This scouting run had led Sally to another important discovery: There were not many items around. She'd only found a few scattered materials and pieces of equipment...

And the only thing she was finding with any regularity was the equipment durability repair item—unique to this map.

If they ran out of the materials for potion crafting, there was little chance they could make more.

"If all our fights are that hard...we'll be out of MP potions by day five."

MP potions generally ran out before HP ones. The kind of spells or skills that could turn the tide of battle generally consumed a lot of MP, and in a battle-focused event like this, they'd be blowing through potions like there was no tomorrow.

And being unable to cast support spells could hurt them on the fifth and final day.

"Hmm...but if we don't rack up points fast, the big guilds'll leave us in the dust. Against anyone that size, I'd want Maple with us...which means we'd have to..."

If they weren't constantly nabbing and keeping orbs, they wouldn't be able to compete with the big guilds.

Sally pondered the issue awhile, and once she'd made up her mind, she pulled a cloak on to disguise herself and dashed off through the trees, hunting for other players.

It didn't take her long to find a party of three. They were sticking to the shadows and undergrowth, like Sally herself had been when she was with Chrome and Kasumi.

From the tree above, Sally listened in for a minute and soon learned they were a scout party.

She checked their weapons—a staff, a greatsword, and a one-handed sword with a shield. Then she moved a short ways out, dropped down to ground level, and headed past them, letting the brush rustle as she moved through it.

She clicked her tongue, feigning irritation at the encounter.

"......! She's solo! Get her!"

"Right! We've got this!"

Three against one.

Sally's look of dismay ensured they wouldn't pass up a fight.

As Sally repeatedly glanced over her shoulder, a spell flew at her. A greatsword charge wasn't far behind.

She dodged the spell, then performed an evasive maneuver, avoiding the charge as well at the cost of balance.

The sword and shield wielder had been waiting for that moment, but she deflected the prepared attack with her dagger and rolled out of the way of the wind blades that followed.

"Leap!"

She used a skill to gain distance, scrambled to her feet, and raised her daggers, edging backward.

Her opponents interpreted that as a signal she was about to flee, and they closed in.

"Leap!"

"Heavy Charge!"

The greatsworder rushed in, and the one-handed sword fighter leaped to her rear, cutting off her escape route. The support spells they were receiving kept up the pressure.

From their perspective, they had her on the ropes.

Just one step away from finishing Sally off.

Then, before they picked up on the fact that she was still evading *everything* they threw at her, she took a tumble through the dirt and broke into a dead run off into the woods.

And in this terrain, they quickly gave up on following her trail.

"Come on, forget about her."

"Yeah, no use searching."

"Good. That went well."

Once she was sure she'd lost her pursuers, Sally set out to find another party and deliberately let herself get seen once more. This all might seem crazy—but Sally had a clear goal in mind. She was maxing out her Sword Dance effect, which would eventually double her STR.

Sword Dance

+1% STR each time you dodge an attack.

Max 100%.

Buff vanishes if you take damage.

Twenty minutes later...

Sally had achieved her goal. Sword Dance was giving her the maximum boost to STR.

"I'm ready. Oboro, come on."

She summoned her white fox and stuck it around her neck. Oboro wrapped its tail around her like a scarf, nuzzling her cheek. Focusing on the task ahead, Sally made her way toward one of the guilds she'd found.

"...All right, orbs confirmed."

There were two midsize guilds, and in both cases, she could see the orb from a distance. But there were plenty of obstacles between her and them, plus a lot of defenders. A frontal assault would be tough. Both bases were set up inside ruins, with a scattering of stone buildings and the orbs placed in the central clearing.

Sally was steadily closing in on the less evenly guarded one.

But they *were* a midsize guild and had no shortage of players to cover a lot of ground.

"*Phew... You got this, Sally!*"

She slapped her cheeks, focused her mind, and plunged into the weakest section of the guild's defensive perimeter.

"Enemy! There's just one!"

A lookout spotted her and alerted the orb's defenders.

"Leap!"

She used a skill to quickly swing left.

"Surround her!"

A portion of the defenders moved to do exactly that—and succeeded. Attacks rained down upon her—

—then she melted into the air, like mist.

The defenders were shocked, but orders to locate her again went out—and Sally was quickly discovered once more, this time on the right.

A second wave rushed to respond. They made swift work of the intruder, pounding away.

And she dissolved just like before.

Working together, Sally and Oboro had used Mirage to gather everyone's attention and create gaps in the guild's defenses. In reality, she'd just walked straight on in, giving her unhindered access to their orb.

"Superspeed!"

By the time the guards noticed, it was too late.

Her skill had allowed her to cover the last bit of ground in a flash and snatch the orb without needing to fight anyone.

Still, escaping would be no easy task. She was surrounded and would have to break through their lines.

"Slash!"

The extra attacks that Chaser Blade gave her combined with the dual daggers buffed by Sword Dance made short work of her opponents, who were still dazed by her initial sprint through their lines.

When the Sword Dance buff was maxed out, Sally's daggers *hurt*.

While Superspeed was still active, Sally struck at everyone within reach, prying a path open.

And her DPS was so high that anyone who stood in her way crumbled.

After scouting out the place, she knew the odds would be against her in a frontal assault. That was why she'd decided an unorthodox approach would probably be her best shot at grabbing their orb.

Her skill set was what made it possible. Flawless evasion and agility were prerequisites to pulling off this strategy.

And it was a plan that worked *because* it was the first day— no one had any real information, and their defenses had yet to be tested.

"Water Wall!"

Throwing up a barrier to keep enemy spells at bay, Sally found the softest point in their now-weakened defense and punched through.

"That definitely won't work twice… Oh, good, here they come!"

No defender would stand idly by when their orb was stolen.

This guild had a fair number out on the attack, but there were still forty of them to deal with.

And now they had no orb to defend. They were *all* on Sally's heels.

She ran.

Right toward the other midsize guild.

Never letting them catch up but never letting them lose sight of her, she ran until the other guild was in sight. This guild had standardized their gear, and all of them were dressed in blue—just like Sally. She figured she could pass as one of them easily enough.

They saw Sally leading an army their way and braced for a fight. Her pursuers naturally thought this was her guild and got ready to launch an all-out attack.

Both were wrong, but the fight was now a foregone conclusion. Sally's goal was to use the chaos of battle to steal a second orb. That's why she'd led the army here.

"Oboro, Fleeting Shadow!"

As the fight began, they quickly lost track of Sally.

Oboro's skill made her invisible for a single second. That was long enough for her to reach some thickets and hide.

The two guilds seemed evenly matched. The army she'd led was hell-bent on getting their orb back, and they were making headway.

The battle was far too furious for anyone to spare a thought for where Sally had gone.

Since the players hounding Sally had all come from the same direction, the defenders were forced to meet them on that side—meaning if she sneaked around the back of their camp, few guards were left to stand in her way.

She carefully threaded through the ruins and took aim.

"...Leap! Double Slash!"

Sally picked an angle with only five defenders and caught them by surprise, cutting them down before they could recover. The Sword Dance buff helped tremendously.

"Got it!"

With the orb in hand, she used her patented evade-and-counter technique to make short work of the survivors before hurrying back to the guaranteed safety of the Maple Tree base.

"If I make it home, Maple's there! Once these orbs are in our base—they aren't going anywhere."

The furious battle would last a while.

It would take some time for them to realize the orb was gone and try to give chase.

More than enough for her to make a clean getaway.

While she ran, Sally sent a message to her guild.

It simply said she'd grabbed some orbs and wanted to hand them off at the entrance.

The idea was to get them safely under Maple's protection as soon as possible, freeing up Sally to hunt for the next one.

This first day was critical.

If they wanted to win, they couldn't afford to waste a second.

"There it is!"

Sally had been careful, making sure there was no one on her tail. She peered out of the underbrush—checking for ambushes—and spotted Chrome waiting for her.

She slipped over to him and deposited the two orbs into his hands.

"Wow...already?"

"...I'm gonna spend the day racking up points. You make sure we hold on to 'em."

"You got it!"

Three guilds had lost their orbs to Maple Tree now. And the location of a guild's own orb was always shown on every member's map.

All three orbs were in the same place.

Would they work together? Or would they give up on recovering their original orbs and gang up on other guilds now that there was no need to devote anyone to defense? Either way, having an orb stolen this early was undoubtedly a wrench in whatever plans they might've had.

"It's go time!"

Not even taking a moment to rest, Sally plunged back into the fray. If she stopped, the large guilds would build up an insurmountable lead.

She'd located more guilds, and she wanted their orbs, too.

Chrome took the orbs from Sally back to the others and placed them on their pedestal.

"Wow, Sally's amazing!"

"Yeah, she made snatching them sound easy, but…nobody else could pull that off."

After a moment of deep admiration, the topic turned toward their security.

They decided Kanade, Mai, Yui, and Maple would be on guard.

"We'll be in the back," Chrome said.

"If you're ever in trouble… Well, you won't be."

"Once things die down, we'll head out to check our surroundings and thin the enemy numbers."

Iz was combat ready and could be included in scouting parties.

"I'd better change up my shield so I can use Crystal Wall."

Maple had no plans to use her attack skills, so she'd be focusing on defense alone—Crystal Wall was great for that. With the relevant shield equipped, she could instantly generate a crystalline barrier, blocking any advance.

"We're sticking to one hammer each."

It was important to hide their true capabilities for as long as possible.

*   *   *

Fifteen minutes later...

Furious players started pouring in. The entire midsize guild, faces like demons, charged forward like an avalanche—and found only four players standing in their way.

No need to close with a party that small. They could just have their mages attack from afar.

But when the spellfire cleared, the defenders were advancing toward them, clearly unharmed. And one of them sported glittering angel wings.

None of them knew what that meant. Most assumed the other team's great shielder had used some skill to block the damage, so they simply moved in to finish the job. No one paid much attention to the two hammer wielders at all, which was perfectly normal.

"Crystal Wall!"

As the intruders raced between the twins, Maple raised a wall. They ran headlong into it and staggered backward—that was their undoing.

""Double Stamp!""

The deafening noise of hammer meeting armor rang out. It took only a single blow to fell each player.

Seeing so many of their front-liners downed in one shot amid a spray of red damage sparks, the rest of the attacking guild was forced to reassess the situation.

These formidable foes were tiny. Cutesy clothes peeked out from beneath their robes. A complete mismatch with the giant hammers and ludicrous damage output.

The attackers froze.

Double Stamp was a normal skill. It only hit twice. Most players should be able to tank both hits just fine.

The mages cast a second round of spells—but once again, their attacks did *nothing.* And any player who didn't dodge fast enough shattered like glass.

But they still had numbers on their side.

They couldn't retreat yet.

These hammerers weren't exactly fast. Nor were they stepping outside the glowing zone generated by the angel skill. Given the size of the room itself, a flanking maneuver was definitely an option.

"Circle around them! Take out the one with wings!"

No sooner did they hear this order than a new voice barked, "Girls, do the thing!"

""Okay!""

The assaulting guild obviously had no idea what to expect.

But the hammer girls ran straight forward, evenly spaced.

"Cover Move! Cover Move!"

And Maple kept pace with them—

—bringing her AOE defense field with her.

"Well, that was dumb. Hit those wings! We'll do extra damage now!"

The attacking guild's great shielder was very familiar with the downsides to Cover Move.

But this approach was perfect for Maple. It meant she could move her glow zone to the enemy back line.

That meant the twins were still under her protection.

"Wait, that's... P-pull back!"

The one who shouted the order earlier had been keeping his distance from the hammer threat—meaning he could see over their shoulders to the back of the room, where the final defender stood... with multiple bookshelves floating around him.

"Shadow Stitch," Kanade whispered.

And for the next three seconds, none of the attackers could move.

"Wha…?! I-I'm stuck…!"

As realization sank in, doom swept toward them.

Two hammers smashed through Magic Barrier unhindered, pulverizing the players beyond.

When the longest three seconds of their lives were over, the back line was in shambles, their commander downed, and the front line was completely penned in.

In mere minutes, four players had wiped them out.

They really should have given up on the orb and gone after some other guild.

And thus, Maple Tree convinced their opponents they were better off fighting one another. It was still early on the first day, but they'd achieved two important goals—securing their own safety and chipping away at the ranks of their foes.

As these fights took place, people were spectating all the action in a town created specifically for the event, also under the same time compression.

Screens had been set up everywhere, letting players watch the event unfold. And it had everything the main stratum towns had—including item shops and training rooms like the one in Maple Tree's guild home.

Event participants were unable to contact anyone outside the combat map, so there was no way for an observer to relay information to those inside.

There was also a unique bracelet item that could be used in this zone that allowed players to step out and come back, with the time differential calculated automatically. Of course, by the time they got back, the event standings might have changed dramatically. Players invested in spectating were unlikely to leave in the first place.

Any event participants who reached the five-death limit would also be sent here.

"Woo, they're going at it!"

"Well worth the watch. Glad we came."

"I figure the big guilds have this in the bag. No way for the little ones to compete."

"Yeah...looks like the crowds here are people like us, who aren't even in guilds. That or guilds who decided it wasn't even worth trying."

"No point if you don't have the numbers. No exceptions."

"Who's gonna come in first? The Order of the Holy Sword or Flame Empire?"

"Those two sucked up all the top rankers. If we're lucky, we'll get to see them duke it out—find out who's strongest!"

Virtually everyone agreed nobody could compete with those two guilds.

"Oh, wait, speaking of small guilds...what about Maple Tree?"

"Yeah...hmm. Hard to say. Too many unknowns. Right?"

Everyone made a face, and then someone said, "Well, they can't beat the big dogs anyway."

"...Yeah. I mean, those guilds have anti-Maple schemes in place. It's hopeless!"

Just then, Maple Tree showed up on-screen. They were fighting groups with far greater numbers and winning without even breaking a sweat. Everyone watching froze.

"...Or not?"

"Still. There's no way...right?"

"...Where'd these crazy hammer girls come from? How the—?"

They were only on-screen long enough to freak the audience out—and then the feed cut away.

◆□◆□◆□◆□◆

The orb thief who'd engineered that whole spectacle was currently studying a small guild at the base of a cliff.

"They're pretty small," Sally observed, peering around a rock.

Currently, she could only see five.

And unless they had a Maple, nobody could defend a base with so few people.

That meant most guilds would be putting the bulk of their members on defense. A team this small made it likely their total head count was similar to Maple Tree.

"I can take 'em."

She slipped out from behind that outcropping, staying hidden as she moved from perch to perch.

A large party would be spotted before long, but a careful solo player could creep surprisingly close.

"Oboro, Fleeting Shadow."

When she ran out of cover, Sally made herself invisible for a single second, using that brief moment to reach the thickets by the base itself.

She listened closely; it didn't sound like anyone had noticed.

She'd scouted the place from above and knew they weren't all constantly looking up—they had one player focused on the cliffs above, while the others watched the narrow trails leading in.

"All right, game time."

Sally quietly stepped out of the bushes and headed for the one keeping an eye on the cliffs above.

She could easily have killed the guard before there was even a chance to make a sound, but she chose to take it slow.

"E-enemy!" went up the yell—and *then* Sally swooped in for the kill.

And because the call had come from the one who'd been on cliff duty, the other players all looked up and broke into a run—right past the bushes where Sally was hiding.

With their attention all drawn upward, they were slow to react as Sally rushed past, low to the ground, daggers slashing all the while.

She held the advantage in levels and gear, and only the last of them even managed to take a swing.

"No chance to let 'em see a skill. Nice. They won't pose a problem even if they do come after me. Let's hit another."

She grabbed their orb and picked a path back up the cliff.

As she moved, she checked her map, thinking fast while keeping one eye on her surroundings. While she had their orb, her latest victims would know exactly where she was, so stopping to think would be too risky.

"Another small crew... No, wait, that one might be rough. Hmm. Maybe I should scout farther? I really wanna find out where the big guilds are."

Her mind made up, she ran off, heading for unexplored realms.

Back at base, the rest of Maple Tree had defense locked down.

The only skill Maple had shown was Martyr's Devotion, and nobody had realized yet that this skill was vulnerable to piercing damage.

Having annihilated all the invaders, Mai and Yui had settled down next to Maple.

"*Hah...hah...* This is hard work!"

"Mm. Phew... It does take a lot out of you."

The twins had handled virtually all the actual combat and were visibly tired.

"I think it'll be a while before anyone else comes," Kanade said. "Given the beating we just handed them, they won't be back for more."

Indeed, the blue guild had already abandoned the idea of recovering their orb.

It was still the first day, so nobody wanted to rack up a second death so soon.

"The others left to hunt down scouting parties, and Sally's... way out there, huh?" Maple said, inspecting her map.

Sally's marker was moving steadily away from the guild base.

Maple closed her map and sighed. "Let's take a rest, then. It's not like anyone will have an easy time sneaking up on us. We'll leave the rest to our friends outside for now."

Maple Tree's grown-up/voice-of-reason squad was currently picking off enemy reconnaissance teams.

"These are good, Iz."

"Right! Doping Seeds are pretty powerful."

They were craftable thanks to the New Frontier skill (itself provided by Iz's unique series gear). Doping Seeds raised one stat by 10 percent, at the cost of 10 percent reduction in a different stat.

Up to five could be used at once, and the effect lasted ten minutes, which was quite long.

However, there was no telling what stats would be affected until crafting was complete. To get the seeds she wanted, a mountain of materials had been required.

But her other skill, Faustian Alchemy, allowed her to trade

gold for materials. She'd exchanged a lot of money for Doping Seed materials, prepping all the seeds her guild would need.

Iz had given Sally ten seeds that lowered VIT and raised AGI.

Chrome got VIT and STR buffs that lowered DEX.

Kasumi got STR buffs that lowered INT.

Kanade got INT buffs that lowered STR.

For Maple, Mai, and Yui, it didn't matter what got lowered, so Iz was able to dump a lot of the extras on them.

The gold she'd spent making all those seeds had been enough to found her own guild—twice.

"Heh-heh… Just make sure all that money doesn't go to waste."

"Absolutely."

Kasumi used Keen Sight to locate more players, prompting her team to circle around and ambush them.

CHAPTER 2

Defense Build and Two Foes

While Maple Tree's grown-ups were making quick work of a scouting party...

Far, far away from any Maple Tree member—

Frederica and Drag were on guard duty in the Order of the Holy Sword's base. This guild had been founded by Pain and Dread after they took the top two slots in the first event, and the number of players—as well as those players' levels—was far higher than Maple Tree's.

"Argh, I wanna go out and fight!" Frederica wailed.

"You know we can't. We're too slow."

Neither of them had put many points in AGI. Drag was six foot two and carried a giant ax, which he kept waving around like he couldn't wait to knock someone's head off with it.

Their guild's scout/attack units were all AGI focused, which ruled Frederica out, too. She turned toward Drag, her blond side ponytail swinging outward.

"Like, I know it's better when defending's boring..."

"Is it?"

Frederica took a seat on a big rock, swinging her legs. She definitely looked bored out of her mind.

The Order was a large guild, so their orb was placed in a hard-to-defend area.

Their base was situated in a rocky area surrounded by open fields. It was hard to see enemies coming until they reached the rocks, and there were a ton of ways in.

The orb pedestal itself had no roof over it, so they had to watch for people who might try leaping down from the rocky overhangs as well.

There were a number of nearby caves, too. While they couldn't hide the orb in them, they were at least good for taking naps.

Just as their boredom peaked, word of an enemy attack came. Both were on high alert immediately, crackling with tension.

"How many?"

"Around sixty! More than we have on defense."

"Nice, they're going all out. We'd better get moving. Pain wouldn't shut up about minimizing casualties."

"Yeah... Let's go mop 'em up."

"Sounds good. Oh, right— Have everyone else back off. We'll handle this."

"B-by yourselves?"

"As if we'll need more?"

The messenger thought this was conceit talking—but there was no arguing with that glare.

When Frederica and Drag reached the front line, they found a party of sixty headed straight toward them.

"Our lookouts do good work."

"Mm."

Drag shouldered his ax, eying the enemy's advance. The moment they stepped in range, he swung.

Naturally, his range reached far beyond any other ax wielder.

"Earth Splitter!"

Over twenty yards ahead of him, twenty-inch-deep gashes appeared in the ground, halting the enemy in their tracks.

The land cracked open underfoot, knocking them off balance.

When Drag fought with Frederica, this type of incapacitation allowed her to maximize her damage.

"Multi-Firebolt!"

Magic circles appeared all around her and shot out arcs of flame.

The still-struggling players were riddled with fiery missiles.

This was Frederica's Multi-Cast at work.

It was a powerful skill that allowed her to spend three times the MP to cast multiple copies of each spell—far more copies than simply casting multiple times would create. The Multi-Barrier she'd used against Sally provided a ridiculous amount of defense.

"Heavy Charge!"

Before her barrage even finished, Drag rushed in.

When he swung that vicious ax, it slammed anyone it hit back into the gashes they'd almost freed themselves from.

"Rahh! Burn Ax!"

Swinging a flaming ax around wildly, Drag wasn't even trying to defend himself, which left him extremely vulnerable—but his DPS made up for that.

Killing everyone who got close meant there wasn't much incoming damage to worry about.

Apparently offense is the greatest defense.

That being said, there were *sixty* attackers.

Drag was soon surrounded and being assailed from all sides.

Even then, he paid no heed to defending himself. His foes were free to nail him with their best skills.

"Multi-Barrier! Multi-Barrier!"

But those skills all bounced off the defenses Frederica threw up—never really affecting Drag's HP in any meaningful way.

He knew Frederica would keep him safe, so he didn't *need* to think about blocking.

"Ground Lance!"

Drag slammed his ax into the ground, and six rock lances shot up around him.

The players who were impaled from below tried to free themselves, but Frederica's magic finished them off before they got the chance to escape.

"Is that all you got?! Ha!"

"Cover!"

A great shielder tried to soak Drag's ax damage, but his swing connected with full effect, sending the shield bearer and the covered player to the ground.

This was Drag's other key skill:

Knockback Bestowal.

Anyone who tried to block his blows would be flung backward; but if they didn't block, he'd make sure it hurt.

"Heavy Charge!"

His follow-up attack took a merciless chunk of HP.

Once he had a foe on the ground, Drag would keep up the pressure, each new blow preventing them from ever rising back to their feet.

It would seem might always makes right.

But this fighting style was useless without the right support—

—which Frederica's constant barrage of support and attack spells provided perfectly.

"Multi-Photon Cannon!"

Four magic circles appeared around her, and a few seconds later—laser fire blanketed the enemy positions.

They were trying to retaliate with their skills, but it was no use if they couldn't even get near her.

And no one could risk turning their backs on Drag to go after her.

That road led straight to death.

DPS this high left no room for bewilderment—and no way to fight back.

""""Water Wall!""""

The enemy forces were losing their nerve and backing off, which made it that much easier to whittle down their numbers. Once they were down to around ten, the survivors finally saw an opening and turned to run.

Drag took a step after them but quickly realized they were faster than him and turned back.

"*Whew*, that was a good workout."

"You're really running me ragged here! Did you see how much work that was?! So reckless!"

"My bad. But it works, am I right?"

"I guess. And you never try anything too clever, which makes my job simple."

When they'd said the two of them could handle this together, pride had definitely been a factor.

But pride came from strength.

And that strength opened the path to victory.

"I've been wondering… Frederica, why is it you never run outta MP?"

"Ha, a girl needs her secrets." She flashed a grin and headed back to the orb.

Drag followed.

"Speaking of reckless," she said. "You'd think they'd know better than to attack *us*."

"We were in a cave. They probably hadn't spotted us yet."

"Oh…fair point. Talk about bad luck! For them."

"Got that right. But, man, I wanna go attack someone already."

Clearly, Drag hadn't gotten his fill of fighting yet. Frederica agreed.

"I wanna go in on—what were they called again? Maple Tree? Those guys. I'm gonna land a spell on her for sure this time."

Sally had managed to emerge from their duel unscathed, and it was still bugging Frederica.

"She dodged your Multi-Firebolt? She as good as they say, then?"

"You'd be giving yourself a hand if you tried to dodge a little yourself, Drag."

"Not my style."

They reached their base and reported their successful defense. This news was met with a blend of respect and envy, and everyone went back to chatting around the orb.

◆□◆□◆□◆□◆

Frederica and Drag were guarding the Order of the Holy Sword's orbs because Dread and Pain were out plundering other guilds for theirs. In the interest of efficiency, each one was targeting different guilds.

Dread and a group of thirty had already nabbed two orbs. At the moment, he was toying with one of his twin daggers while poring over a map.

He wasn't exactly built for large-scale battle, so he'd lost a few followers in the process, but it was going pretty well, all things considered.

Dread had lightweight gear, which complemented his dodge-heavy fighting style. That made him mostly autonomous as a fighter, and in an event like this, the other guild members mostly wound up serving as his backup.

"Should we get one more lick in? ...This is getting a bit boring."

He glanced in the direction of their next target, about to head that way.

That's when he spotted a solo player standing there.

Instinctively, he *knew*.

".........Kids, change of plans. Take these orbs and go home. Now."

Nobody knew what to make of that, but they picked up on the urgency in his voice and did as they were told.

When they were gone, the robed player moved in.

Dread drew his other dagger.

"You're *good*, huh?" he said.

"Am I?"

"......I trust my hunches. They've served me well so far..."

He let out a long breath, focusing his mind.

"That's why, even though I really don't wanna...," he muttered, "...I've gotta take you out while I can."

"I'll admit, I wasn't expecting to see *you* here," Sally said, her blue daggers emerging from her robe.

Dread's eyes narrowed at the sight of them.

"...*Tch*, you're clearly a much bigger threat than Frederica said."

He muttered those words under his breath, but Sally's ears still caught it.

And it helped her choose an approach.

Though these two titans only met by chance, their clash had already begun.

Neither Dread nor Sally opened with any attack skills.

Those ran through a predetermined set of motions, which left the user exposed. Any dual dagger wielder needed to stay agile at all times.

Dread parried Sally's strike, and she easily evaded his.

He had the advantage of speed and was attacking more often, not giving her a chance to hit back.

"Superspeed!"

And he was the first to go for broke.

With his speed buffed, he saw Sally dodge a moment too late and was about to press the advantage—

"......?!"

But before he fully committed to the thrust, he changed his mind, leaping back.

".........Another hunch of yours?"

"If I doubted a single one, I'd be dead."

Instinct alone had stopped him.

He'd sensed Sally had evasion techniques beyond his own.

He looked her over again, keeping his distance.

"I knew I was gonna have to take you out here...Godspeed!"

This skill doubled as Dread's nickname. It was what granted him his supernatural speed.

Since human perceptions couldn't keep up with something moving so fast, it meant he literally vanished for ten whole seconds.

"...Huh."

Sally had done her homework and knew about the skill.

Dread hadn't kept it secret for one simple reason: Knowing about it didn't help you counter it.

Only a handful of players in the game stood a chance against him.

But…Sally was one of them.

"Waterflow!"

She tracked her invisible opponent by sound and the disturbance in the air caused by his passing, intentionally leaving a fatal opening to lead his attack.

Then she yelled the name of a skill that didn't exist—the same one she'd shown Frederica—and parried his attack with her dagger.

"Leap!"

She bounded away, buying herself time to gauge his next approach, but Dread never showed.

"…He left? Well, at least I got to show off Waterflow again."

Confident he was in the same guild as Frederica, Sally decided selling them on the fake information was benefit enough.

"……Dread's gonna be pretty hard to hit. Those hunches of his—if I did that, I guess I'd go with fear? Like an instinctive danger sense."

Relying on instinct to detect threats was a perfectly legitimate technique, and Sally wanted to try it out herself—so she headed to find another guild.

While he was catching up with his squad, Dread reviewed their clash.

"Waterflow, huh? She's plenty dodgy even without that. And it felt like…"

Dread had only encountered two other players that made him shudder.

One was Pain…and the other, Maple.

"If she's on their level…how did I get away in one piece?"

Sally still had hidden talents—he was sure she'd been holding back. She wouldn't have been strong enough to make him shudder otherwise.

After that unsettling thought, he decided it was no use mulling it over.

"I'll talk to Pain when I get back. He's the smart one."

Giving up on trying to figure it out on his own, he scratched his head, narrowing his eyes.

"Guess I'll suggest we take 'em out on our terms."

He had the face of a man who knew exactly who he needed to kill.

The unexpected clash had given both parties something to chew on.

Dread had come away with a sense that there was much more to Sally than Frederica's report had indicated.

Sally had successfully shored up the idea that Waterflow actually existed, and…she had discovered a lead on how to improve her evasion even more.

Wanting to build experience with this new approach, Sally crushed another nameless small guild.

She'd also grabbed another orb between her attack on the cliff-side guild and her clash with Dread.

In other words—she was currently carrying three.

It was high time she swung by the Maple Tree base.

"The first orb we grabbed oughtta be scoring us some points soon."

The opening hours of this event had seen a lot of combat.

The big guilds were naturally dominating, but the midsize guilds were pulling every trick in the book to stay competitive.

Small guilds were all struggling—with one notable exception.

Time in the compressed zone had started at what appeared to be noon. The sun would be setting shortly.

With the reduced visibility, each guild would get even more aggressive.

And Sally would use the darkness to mount even bolder assaults.

"Better get on home."

While Sally was racing back, the rest of her guild were wiping out another group of unfortunate souls.

There were only three opponents, so Mai and Yui had taken care of them with the iron spheres.

""Maple! We got a new skill!""

"Oh, wow! That's awesome!"

Neither had any intention of keeping their skills a secret from Maple, so they quickly told her the effect and acquisition conditions.

Farshot

Attack distant foes with a shock wave.

Conditions

Kill a set number of enemies with Throw.

The effect was just like the name implied. Swing a sword, and a slashing attack would project outward; swing a hammer, and it'd produce a circular shock wave.

The damage these ranged attacks inflicted was significantly less than an ordinary attack, but with Mai and Yui, even that reduced amount was enough to one-shot most things.

"You two wanna try it in the next fight?"

"Let's not. Sally said we should keep our cards close to our chests. It'd be nice if we could try it out a bit in back, though."

"Go right ahead!" Maple said.

Mai and Yui left the defensive line briefly to familiarize themselves with their new skill. They were back before long.

The twins looked pumped—clearly pleased to have a new way to contribute.

"Heads up. Our friends are on the way home," Kanade announced, glancing at his map.

He'd only burned the one grimoire—Shadow Stitch—and Maple had stuck to only providing support (with Martyr's Devotion). They were still fully stocked for the coming night's challenges.

That was all thanks to the twins' hard work.

Naturally, the two of them were getting quite tired.

They kept collapsing to the ground each time they fought off a new wave and clearly wouldn't last much longer.

"Sally'll be back soon, and so will Chrome. You two can go rest awhile," Maple suggested. "You must be exhausted."

The twins both nodded and headed down the back passage. They were motivated but had reached their limits.

It was important to rest while they had the chance.

"Are you fine not taking a break, Kanade?"

"I haven't really moved much."

After Maple and Kanade chatted for a bit, Chrome appeared.

"Kasumi and Iz are mopping up a small guild," he said.

"Do they need help?"

"Nah, Iz is crafting bombs like crazy, and Kasumi is rolling them down the cave. It shouldn't take 'em long."

This was an approach only Iz could possibly come up with. On the other hand, even if anyone else was capable of it and tried that approach on Maple Tree's cave, Maple's skill would've made them all immune to explosions. It would just be very loud.

"I figured I'd be more useful on defense."

"Mai and Yui were pretty worn out, so this is great timing!"

They now had the two best great shielders in the game holding down the fort.

Both of them gave new meaning to the phrase *hard to kill.*

With their defense all but unassailable, the rest of Maple Tree was free to focus entirely on offense.

That was why Kasumi and Iz were taking it slow and steady.

"Keep 'em going."

"You got it."

Megabombs.

These could usually only be crafted in workshops—but Iz could make them anywhere.

And since she could spend money to pull materials out of thin air, Iz had come prepared with as much cash as she could muster, allowing her to make a ton of Megabombs.

Kasumi took those bombs and kept hurling them into the cave entrance.

The passage was on a downslope, so the explosives were carried away by gravity, and a short while later, they'd hear them explode.

At first, there were lots of screams, but these were fading.

"...Did we get them all?"

"I'll take point." Kasumi kept her katana high as they headed in.

The orb room was covered in scorch marks left by the bombardment. There was one surviving player, swaying on their feet, sword in hand.

"First Blade: Heat Haze."

Kasumi activated a skill that propelled her forward, striking the player down before there was even a chance for them to react.

"Whew... Works on everyone but Sally."

Sally had ducked under it, but in Kasumi's experience, nobody else had been able to dodge it, much less immediately connect their evasive maneuver with a counter.

And being able to handle any type of foe was a big part of Kasumi's and Chrome's fighting styles.

Kasumi was Maple Tree's most "normal" fighter; she had a stable style precisely because it didn't depend on anything clever or convoluted. If she was stronger, she'd win. Her approach to combat lacked any obvious weaknesses foes could exploit.

She was the least likely to give Iz or Chrome any heart attacks.

But to her foes, she was merciless and strong beyond reason.

"Let's grab the orb and bring it home. We don't want to be here when they're all done reviving."

"Sounds like a plan."

Kasumi pocketed the orb, and they left the cave.

It wasn't flashy, but they were steadily netting wins for their team while eliminating the chance of any unfortunate mishaps.

The current standings were dominated by the big guilds—and one small guild. The two biggest guilds, the Order of the Holy Sword and Flame Empire, were one step ahead of everyone else. Maple Tree was nipping right at their heels.

Flame Empire was guarding their orb in a grassy field, the open, flat terrain only broken up by a few stray trees.

On duty were "Trapper" Marx, eighth place in the first event, and "Saint" Misery, who'd come in tenth.

Misery specialized in AOE support, but she was also good at AOE attacks. She could hurt or heal however she wished.

Marx had made extensive use of traps in the first event but managed to keep that fact a secret—until some loose-lipped guild members accidentally leaked it to Frederica.

That was the downside of working in large groups: Loose lips sink ships.

As his moniker implied, Marx knew a lot of spells that could function like traps. They could produce an array of effects, from bursts of smoke to pillars of fire. And they'd activate if any non-ally—anyone not in his guild or party—stepped into range.

The downside was that he had to place them beforehand. Since this wasn't great for offensive tasks, he'd been stuck on guard duty.

Their attack teams were led by the fourth place "Flame Empress" Mii and the seventh place "Splinter Sword" Shin.

"Are we gonna be all right? They're not gonna get through my traps, are they?"

"It'll be fine. Even if they get through, we can count on our team."

Judging from the looks this comment drew, the "team" was actually counting on the two of them to make sure everything was okay.

"I can't stop worrying... What if we lose our orb? Will everyone be mad at me?"

Marx kept pacing around the orb in question, but for all his concerns, the traps he'd laid were brutally effective. They were nigh impossible to spot until they activated, and once they did, almost nobody could walk away unscathed.

And since he'd placed a lot of them—and placed them well—Marx was eliminating a *lot* of enemies.

As pillars of fire reared up and explosions roared, it was easy to tell what path the enemy was taking.

"See? Another wave of invaders, torn to bits. Your traps work!"

"Huh… Well, that's a relief!"

The battered survivors were easily eliminated by the remaining guild members, buffed by Misery's support magic.

Once that was done, several guards escorted Marx out to replace the traps that had been activated.

"Uh…is this spot good? Hmm. And maybe over there?"

Watching him mutter away as he set more traps, his teammates wondered how these were so effective.

It looked like he was just setting traps haphazardly…but players seemed to *always* walk right into them.

Maybe it had to be chalked up to pure talent.

Just as Sally had a knack for evasion and Maple had a talent for discovering weird interactions and Dread had a keen sense for things.

Most of the game's top players had *some* sort of quirk that set them apart.

And Marx's gift for trap placement was another example of this in action.

A natural sensitivity.

When he was finished placing traps, he retreated to the pedestal.

There were fewer players attacking now. Marx looked relieved.

"Something's coming!" Misery shouted.

Marx spun around, looking where she was pointing. A whole mess of fire and explosions marked the spot.

While he panicked, she quickly yelled, "I'll go take a look!" and ran off, five guild members in tow.

What they found was a single player, appearance hidden beneath a robe.

Misery couldn't believe her eyes.

The robed intruder was stepping on traps, then instantly leaping back, like it was obvious something had been set there.

"Hmm...a fear radar... Gotta up the accuracy... Won't be easy."

And with that cryptic mutter, she turned and walked away.

".............We're saved."

"Wh-what do you mean?"

"Come on! Who was that monster? Was that a skill? Or just... talent?!"

Counting her blessings, Misery headed back to Marx and escorted him as he anxiously reset the traps.

"Here...no, they might get through again...ahhh..."

"Don't worry. That player was one of a kind."

"Are you sure...?"

Even as they spoke, flames roared on the other side of the passage. The unmistakable sound of players dying helped Marx settle down and focus on his work.

As for the Flame Empress herself—

—Mii stood at the head of a party, approaching her foes. They all had swords raised.

"Step aside, and we shall spare your lives."

Mii's voice cut through air crackling with tension.

This, however, was not a proposal the orb's defenders could accept.

"Attack!" The front ranks launched themselves at her.

Mii's weapon was a staff.

Her red cloak was certainly eye-catching, but it was clearly something a back-liner would wear, which meant it probably offered little in the way of protection.

"Flame Empress," she whispered.

Two fireballs appeared around her, each a yard in diameter. Manipulating their movements with her hands, she used these fiery missiles to dominate her foes.

Despite her class, Mii was first into the fray because that allowed her to do the most damage:

Literally incinerating her foes.

"Foolish. How foolish."

The confidence with which she tore through enemies was spellbinding.

"Eruption."

The ground exploded. Great gouts of fire spewed forth.

Mii could control fire at will, and this meant she had a lot of flashy moves.

Her might was fully on display, and the sheer spectacle of destruction made her foes falter.

"Detonate."

Anyone who was unlucky enough to survive her firestorm was hit by a low-damage, high-knockback blast.

This was overwhelming strength.

But it was hardly cost-efficient.

Big spells came with a steep price.

This was why the twenty players behind her had their inventories stuffed to the brim with MP potions. Her personal resupply squad.

"Ha... So that was all you had. We're done here."

When the last foe crumbled to ash, her fireballs vanished.

"Your MP potion."

"Mm-hmm."

Mii accepted the offering, downed it, and let out a sigh.

"Secure the orb."

"Right away."

She closed her eyes, savoring the victory—a fatal error.

Sally was watching all this go down from her hiding spot. For all her talk about heading home, she'd been unable to resist a detour to see Mii's squad in action.

"Gaaahhh?!"

Hearing that cry, Mii opened her eyes in time to see the player on orb duty vanish in a puff of light while a mysterious robed figure raced off with their prize.

"! She's strong... I can tell. Take the orbs we've gathered and head back to base! Little sense in risking all our lives!"

The power in her bark instilled the fear of death in her squad, and they turned and ran, taking the rest of their haul back to safety. When she was sure they were moving, Mii chased after the robed figure.

"Flare Impetus!"

Flames shot out of Mii's soles, and she rocketed after the robed figure— But not much later, she lost sight of her entirely.

Sally had taken advantage of a convenient corner to activate Fleeting Shadow.

By the time Mii was frantically trying to figure out where her quarry had scurried off to, Sally was long since gone.

Mii kept the search up for a while, then flopped down on the ground.

"Augh...! I blew it! It's all my faaaault...!"

This Mii was anything but the regal powerhouse she had been earlier.

Her dignified authority had vanished, and all that remained was a kid fretting over her blunder.

"Why did I decide to role-play...?"

Yes, Mii had just been acting out a character of her own creation.

She'd stumbled on a number of powerful skills and, before she knew it, found herself the center of attention. Too embarrassed to just be herself, she wound up creating a fictional persona and had lived to regret it.

The victory she'd been savoring was actually...simply getting through the fight without letting the facade slip.

"Ughh...this sucks. Dammit, now I'm gonna have to go crush another guild on my way back."

She was lashing out in frustration.

But Mii had the strength to do that without fear of the consequences.

And while she was searching for Sally, she stumbled upon a midsize guild—the perfect size for her.

"I've gotta at least bring back *one* orb. If I see that robe again, I'm gonna set it on fire!"

Explosions going off all around her, Mii charged into the enemy guild base as towers of flame erupted from the ground and fireballs wheeled through the air—she even threw out a Custom Numbing Trap that Marx had given her. It wasn't long before the midsize guild was no more.

Mii's immense firepower made this possible, but the current

49

event format played to her strengths. Not everyone who'd done well in the first event could solo a whole guild.

It was likely only Mii, Pain, and Maple who could manage it reliably.

Mii pocketed the new orb and, with another outpouring of fire, set off for the Flame Empire base.

"There you are, Mii!" Marx cried, relieved.

He'd been pacing anxiously around the orb pedestal again.

The rest of her squad had brought their haul back ahead of her return.

"One more for the pile," Mii announced. "Sadly, not the one that was snatched from right under our noses."

They'd seen her crush guilds on her own already, but the news still caused a stir.

"We'll head out once more anon. Prepare yourselves!"

""""As you command!""""

This enthusiastic response made Mii really reluctant to go.

This time, Sally actually did head back to Maple Tree.

If the orbs she was holding were captured by anyone else, all the points would be theirs. That was a risk she didn't want to take.

"I got real lucky on the last one, too."

She'd only managed to slip in because Mii had let her guard down.

"Gotta cover as much ground as possible on day one..."

Sally was gonna push herself to the limit to ensure she and Maple won.

All unaffiliated event participants were automatically placed into ad hoc guilds. Predictably, many of these players had their fun and hit their five-death limits. They were starting to filter into the crowds in the spectators' zone—

—and telling everyone how they'd been taken out.

"Come on, this is too soon!"

"Well, we knew from the start we weren't gonna do anything crazy in a makeshift guild. I just wanted to see the best players with my own eyes!"

"Odd goal, but I guess that makes sense. So? You take out at least one?"

The defeated player meekly looked at the floor. "I...think that would be a lot to ask of anyone *normal*."

The crowd sighed. They had been hoping for an upset.

"Didn't become a hero, then?" someone asked, feigning deep sadness. They gave the man a pat on his shoulders.

"Yeah, I knew it was impossible! I knew that going in, but... Going up against those guys is impossible. You take a swing at Pain, he parries it flawlessly. There're no openings! It's like he has eyes on the back of his head."

He would have at least liked to land a single blow, but while he was still griping, the conversation had already moved on.

"Speaking of eyes on the back of heads—what's up with that Sally? The girl from Maple Tree? She took me down once."

"Oh, the roaming field boss?"

Several players present remembered the nightmare that occurred during the second event.

"She's not roaming this time. I was walking through a forest, and she swung out of a tree and cut my head off."

"...Is she descended from a ninja clan?"

"Seeing someone like her makes you wanna try out new moves. I was almost glad I died!"

The man certainly seemed cheery as he reminisced.

Since someone mentioned a certain guild, a few people got curious about their current standing in the event.

"Maple Tree is...doing all right. If nothing else, they're definitely the top small guild."

"Gonna be hard to hit the top ranks, though. Just not enough people."

The conversation drifted back to the eliminated players—who'd killed them and what the big guild strategies might look like.

Sally had arrived at Maple Tree's cave.

"I'm back!"

Mai and Yui were out collecting the iron spheres they'd hurled at attackers.

Maple had come along to help but quickly realized she literally couldn't do anything.

The spheres were so heavy even Kasumi could barely lift them, so it was only natural that when Maple tried, they didn't even budge.

"Oh! There you are, Sally!"

"I brought back...*four* orbs!"

""""Wow!!""""

The extreme build trio all looked impressed. If they could keep these safe, they'd get a huge point bump.

Chrome and Kanade heard the cries and came out to join them.

And not long after, Kasumi and Iz came back from their scouting run.

*   *   *

They'd stolen eight orbs in all.

Three of them had reached the three-hour defense requirement and were already back on the original guild's pedestal.

The first orb Sally, Kasumi, and Chrome had nabbed together, and the other two orbs Sally had pilfered by setting two midsize guilds against each other.

Kasumi and Iz had brought back one orb, and Sally had brought back four.

From this point on, they had to guard these five and their own orb, meaning no one could let their guards down anytime soon.

But the game's most powerful tank was on guard duty.

You could count the players that stood a chance against her on the fingers of one hand.

"Oh, yeah— I should mention I just made off with these orbs, so most likely the owners will come after them sooner than later. They were all from small guilds, though."

"No matter how many times I hear it, I dunno how you manage it," Kanade said.

"Oh, speak of the devil!" Chrome drew his weapon and moved to the entrance. But the stream of players coming down the hall clearly had more numbers than a single small guild.

Knowing they were at a disadvantage, Sally's victims had decided to team up.

There was little advantage in betraying one another so early; their interests aligned right up until they were sure they could get the orbs back.

As the players streamed in, they saw six orbs waiting.

And only eight players defending.

Their impromptu alliance wasn't exactly the epitome of

coordination, but there *were* fifty of them. Anyone could see they had a huge numbers advantage.

Seeing the pile of loot within eyeshot got them worked up, too. Quite a few schemers were already thinking about how to turn on their allies the moment the defenders were dealt with.

Luck was on their side.

Just take out eight players for a shot at a six-orb haul.

They might never get a deal this good again.

They all charged in, roaring at the tops of their lungs.

Spells flew, and dust clouds swirled.

But even as their bloodshot eyes drew near, the defenders seemed unperturbed.

"Is this the first time all eight of us have fought together?"

"I think so. At least, since Iz joined the front lines."

"Maple, do your thing," Chrome said.

His companions knew immediately what he meant. So far, this was *all* Maple had been required to do in this event.

"Aye-aye! Martyr's Devotion!"

"One Heal, coming right up!"

This skill sacrificed a chunk of Maple's HP, but Kanade quickly topped it back up without missing a beat.

As Maple moved forward, the other seven followed. The two forces clashed head-on.

Mai and Yui were taking blows from all directions, but nothing even remotely hurt them.

""Double Stamp!""

There was a resounding *thud*, and then players went flying. A short distance away, a cleaver and a katana were cutting and carving open a path.

"Hrah!"

"Hmph."

A few clever players dodged their attacks, focusing on reaching the orbs.

But those who stepped out of the glowing zone and ran toward the prize were met with an explosive surprise.

"Aren't you naughty? Those orbs are *ours*."

With Maple at her side, Iz was no different from any other combatant.

She was a legitimate threat.

And anyone who made it through her barrage was introduced to Kanade's library.

"Paralyze Laser."

A low-powered beam with a high chance of causing an ailment swept horizontally across the room.

The status effect was a powerful one, so even if the range was relatively narrow, no one could discount it.

And even if Kanade didn't finish them off, someone else would—specifically the same girl who'd stolen their orbs in the first place.

"Gah...*gurgle!*"

"D-dammit!"

Players caught by the laser tried to escape, but their movements became sluggish at best.

"And you're outta here!"

Sally was busy sending all the players Kanade paralyzed back to their guilds.

And even as she did, Kasumi, Chrome, Mai, and Yui were all making short work of the front-line attackers.

In the blink of an eye, the alliance had crumbled. The attackers were losing their nerve, and many were turning to run.

*　　*　　*

Some, however, were still hoping to get some hits in.

"Leap!"

A player bounded through a gap between Chrome and Kasumi, clearly not planning on making it back alive.

He swung his blade down, trying to land a hit on the girl in the back with the angel wings.

"Defense Break!"

"Pierce Guard!"

This negated the armor-piercing skill completely.

Despite pouring every ounce of strength into that swing and battle cry, it had been mercilessly rejected, and the blow bounced off the angel without any apparent effect.

Sensing two hurtling hammers coming closer with every second, the last thing the attacking player saw was a glimpse of the face that had been hidden from view the whole time beneath that hood.

"*Maple?* Well, that explains it."

There was resignation in that voice—then the hammers connected.

Not a single attacker would ever touch an orb.

It was a total rout.

But they were lucky. They were the first players to see Maple Tree fully assembled and fighting as one. When the event was over, they would be able to dine out on that story for a while, telling everyone how they'd fought the most terrifying party in the entire game.

As the fighting wore on, the skies grew dark, bringing the hour of day that best suited assassinations and stealth raids.

CHAPTER 3

Defense Build and the Night

A dagger drove home, turning another player into many motes of light.

Three hours had passed since sunset.

Maple Tree had no problem keeping their orbs safe and earned points from each of them.

It wasn't long before Sally slipped out again, racing across the map once more.

In a short while, she'd stolen two more orbs.

And killed countless players.

She'd just taken out another.

"*Whew*, nine o'clock? I wonder how many more orbs I can get before dawn?"

She checked her map.

It was positively bristling with information: locations of weapon repair items, landmarks, guild size, and defenses, as well as core roster size, paths that enemy scouts often took, good locations for ambushes, etc.

*   *   *

The event had been going for nine hours now.

The info she'd gathered was helping her slip through the gaps in the other guilds' defenses.

The reason Sally was going all out on day one was because she wanted to snatch as many orbs as possible while easy foes were still around. In the second half of the event, contests over orbs would get far more intense.

By the final day, it was entirely possible all small guilds would be eliminated, meaning their orbs would no longer be up for grabs.

"Getting an early lead and keeping it is the only way to win."

That was why Sally never stopped running.

She was more than ready for any challenge or threat.

"Next is... Yeah, it's gotta be them."

She was off again.

By this point, alliances were forming, and scouts she'd killed were spreading word about her.

Back at the Maple Tree headquarters, the twins were talking.

"Mai, we still can't dodge normal attacks at all."

"True. But we're most familiar with daggers, so I feel like we should be able to dodge those at least once."

They'd been training with Sally, so they'd seen her weapon in action more than any other. Plus, it was certainly easier to tell where an attack was coming from with a dagger compared with other kinds of weapons.

But that was only relatively speaking—they were pretty far from reliably dodging anything.

"That's why I was wondering if there's a strategy that can take advantage of our strengths."

During the full-team fight, Yui had seen everyone putting their unique talents on display, and it had inspired her to see if there was anything else they could try.

Everyone else would likely say they were plenty unique already, but at their age, they wanted to find something all their own that could help everyone out.

"Hmm, I get that."

"And so I thought of this one thing…," Yui whispered in Mai's ear.

Her idea made Mai's eyes go wide—but it *did* seem like something they could pull off. They looked at each other and grinned.

"That sounds amazing! I love it!"

"Right? If we can pull it off with the right timing…"

"Exactly!"

They started discussing the finer details of their scheme.

Kanade, Maple, and Chrome were watching from across the room.

"I think I'm gonna make a scouting run," Kanade said. "I'll be back in say…two hours?"

"Yeah? Fine by me." Maple nodded immediately.

They had plenty of defenders. And as long as he came back on time, it wouldn't impact their sleep rotation.

She had no reason to say no.

It was Kanade's first time outside the base since the event began, and he first checked his map.

"If Sally's info is right, I should head this way."

Kanade was half scouting, half hoping to collect some orbs himself.

Sally had shared her information-overload map with him

following the all-hands battle, and he remembered every single detail.

"She's pushing herself. I gotta do what I can to help."

Even Sally couldn't keep that up indefinitely. Kanade felt the best way to give her time to rest was if he could snag some orbs himself.

He headed toward his chosen target and hid in the trees, having spotted the orb glittering in the dark once he arrived.

"A midsize guild calls for…"

He used his Sorcerer's Stacks skill to call up his bookshelves and pored over his grimoire collection, ultimately selecting two.

"I should be able to get back faster than I thought. Giant's Arm!"

In response to his call, one of the grimoires flew up, transforming his right arm.

For a short time, his arm would be long and thick.

It was hard to control and didn't last long—definitely not designed for detail work.

But…

It was more than enough to grab an orb off a pedestal seven yards away.

"Flare Impetus."

Flames shot from his feet, and he headed back home, orb in hand.

"A-after that guy!! Noooow!"

The shouts in his wake soon faded. He ran between trees and rocks, quickly gaining ground.

An attack too unexpected for anyone to react in time had allowed him to bring treasure back to the forbidden realms.

"I hope this eases her burden."

Knowing full well Sally was still out there running her feet off, Kanade made it back home safely.

While Kanade was swiping that orb, Sally was, once again, attacking a small guild under cover of darkness.

"Oboro, it's go time."

With her fox around her neck, she quietly moved closer.

This base was outdoors and using a number of torches or similar items to keep things bright; their light could be spotted from miles away.

This made them an obvious target, but they had to keep it bright because of players like Sally.

And Sally could tell more players were patrolling or standing on lookout.

"They've got…fifteen."

She could probably take them all out, but she preferred to avoid combat.

This was mostly to avoid unwarranted attention, but there was also a part of her that was aware active combat would wear her out faster.

When the lookout turned his back, Sally broke into a run.

"Superspeed!"

She *was* definitely getting tired, but she could still compensate by concentrating harder.

She made a beeline for the orb, cutting down anyone who stood in her way and defending herself with magic.

She'd been making these runs all day, polishing her motions until no wasted actions remained. Sally had always been good. Now it would take more than unremarkably strong players to impede her progress.

"Leap!"

She kicked off the ground, hand shooting straight to the orb.

Once she was sure it was in her inventory, she bounded over the pedestal and kept running without slowing down.

She couldn't risk stopping.

Including her latest orb, she had three on her.

There was a perpetual risk of her pursuers catching up.

"*Phew...next!*"

She needed to get as many orbs as possible, as fast as possible.

Sally wasn't stopping, and nobody could stop her.

"Oboro, Fox Fire!"

A few members of that last guild were giving chase, but her pet's flames made them flinch back, increasing her lead.

Slower players were usually stuck on guard duty. That was why Maple was guarding Maple Tree's base.

So once she had the orb, a player like Sally was in the wind.

Keep chasers from catching up, lose them in the darkness, and while they were checking the orb's location on their maps, get far enough away that they would never catch her.

And if they were still on her heels, she could bait them into fighting another guild again.

"Where to go next? ...Hmm?"

She caught a glimpse of torchlight out of the corner of her eye.

There wasn't a single visible guard. A very short-staffed guild, perhaps?

"That looks like a chance...!"

She changed course, aiming for their orb.

Well aware this could be a trap, she swiftly closed in—and was genuinely surprised to find that she didn't bump into anyone.

"...Did a stolen orb just respawn? The terrain says they're mid-size, so..."

If their members started flooding back, it could spell trouble, so Sally made herself scarce.

◆□◆□◆□◆□◆

Maple Tree was busy defending the orb Kanade had swiped.

"Crystal Wall!"

Since Maple could get hit without taking damage, she really hadn't found much use for this skill before, but it was really pulling its weight in this event.

Throwing up an obstacle and stopping foes in their tracks made them sitting ducks for her team's attacks. This thinned their numbers to the point where the front-liners—immortal thanks to Martyr's Devotion—could take them all down.

Maple's support was unbeatable. Mai and Yui were getting hit plenty, and even Chrome often found himself surrounded.

But instead of crumbling, the melee fighters stood their ground, focusing on damage over evasion, and quickly dispatched the attackers. While Maple Tree members almost never needed to dodge, their assailants couldn't afford to let a single blow connect or they'd be done for.

The resulting imbalance was devastating. The defense could throw out so much more damage.

If you couldn't beat Maple, then defeat was inevitable.

"*Whew*, looks like we're done for now."

"Yes...looks like..."

"I'm so tired..."

"The first day's almost over. Should we start taking turns to sleep?"

Chrome had his menu open, and it was indeed almost midnight.

Everyone readily agreed to his suggestion.

Sally, Iz, and Kasumi were all out hunting, so they'd take their turn resting later; given the numbers, it made sense to have two members taking brief naps at a time.

"Mai and Yui, you wanna go first? It's probably best if I stay here."

"Mm...I can cover while you're out, Maple," Kanade said. "I've got some AOE support, too. But for now, I agree—you two can go first."

The twins had the least experience fighting other players and were the defense team's core DPS, so they were already at the peak of fatigue.

They could definitely use a break.

"Okay, go catch some z's! Don't worry, defense is kinda my thing."

The twins came off the front line to sleep.

"Iz and Kasumi will be back soon enough."

That would give them more defensive options. This was undoubtedly the best time for Mai and Yui to get some rest.

"It's only gonna get rougher from here on out."

At this hour, every guild had fewer defenders.

Whether they chose to take advantage of that and focus on attacking or lock down their defenses would depend on their guild's size and their current point count.

Maple Tree needed to keep growing their score while also never letting their defense slacken—with only eight members total.

"Gotta hang in there. I have to protect everyone so we can survive till day five. We can do this."

Maple braced herself for whatever the rest of the night had in store for them.

One AM.

After the full team battle at the base, Sally had been snatching orbs without stop, never once heading home.

She had amassed quite a bit. Her inventory was currently stuffed with *ten* orbs.

That alone was unprecedented, but since orb acquisition wasn't her only goal, heading back had not been an option.

And this secondary goal was almost complete. Sally was leaning against a tree, looking tired. Oboro pressed up against her feet, appearing concerned, and she managed a weak smile, then knelt down to rub its head.

"*Whew...* Maybe it's time I headed back."

She forced herself to run once more.

If she stopped, the players chasing after her would catch up. Being hunted was now a constant for her.

"......Hmm?"

Sally paused for a moment and hid behind a rock. She focused her mind once more, taking stock of the players around her.

This was no small party.

There were more than a hundred people.

"I'm surrounded...!"

Exhaustion had affected her enemy-detection skills without her realizing it.

Her foes were spread out, lurking in the shadows—but the way they were moving made it clear they all knew where she was.

"...One of these orbs belongs to a big guild, huh?"

That would explain it.

Since there was no way to tell which, however, she couldn't dump that orb to make a getaway.

"They're not just gonna *let* me slip away."

She quickly popped her map open, checking the position of Maple Tree's members. Then after sending one quick message, she pulled out five Doping Seeds.

"Right. Gotta make it home somehow."

Even as she spoke, the sky lit up like it was noon.

Someone's spell had installed a miniature sun up above, preventing her from slipping away under cover of darkness.

The players surrounding her were playing for keeps.

"...They must think they've lucked into a big score," Sally whispered, gulping down the last of the Doping Seeds as she emerged from her hiding spot.

Her opponents had quit hiding, too, and were already circling her.

They were leaving some gaps, giving themselves room to fight, but making sure to not present her with any openings she could slip through.

"We've got her cornered! Go!"

They raised a cry, ready to charge—but nobody moved.

"Cornered? Am I?"

Sally's entire demeanor had changed.

This wasn't just *focused*.

She was radiating pure bloodlust.

One false move and they were dead. That's what the dangerous glint in her eyes and her unhinged smile said.

Her foes were starting to believe the odds were actually stacked against *them*.

Sally herself could feel her fatigue vanishing. Surpassing your limits gives you access to unprecedented power.

Her senses were honed, and her body felt light—

"All right...time to do my best to survive."

Whipping herself up, Sally raised her daggers.

Nobody was coming after them, and Maple was getting bored. Then a message came.

"From Sally? What does it say?"

Just three words.

Might die. Sorry.

Nothing more.

Sally could feel her senses working overtime.

And the more she fought, the more they were picking up.

Her ears caught a certain voice barking orders.

"Frederica..."

Not a voice Sally would ever mistake.

And if Frederica was here, she was obviously fighting the Order of the Holy Sword.

That meant Sally had a solid chance at surviving.

"Attack Lure!"

Sally dodged the first wave of spells. The front line seized the moment and surged forward.

They all had the same intel.

If Sally was gonna survive this, she had to stealthily guide the battle.

Fail to control the enemy and she was as good as dead.

"Thanks, Frederica."

With a muttered word of gratitude to her unseen foe, Sally dodged the swings of the front-liners.

"Attack Lure!"

Players in earshot were still attacking, but their blows weren't nearly as strong. Encountering the unexpected sparks surprise and confusion, which dulls attacks.

They didn't realize yet that Sally's skills had no use limit.

In fact, the "skill" simply didn't exist. Blows kept raining down, but Sally was dodging them all manually.

"Wow...I can see everything."

The change in perception was astonishing.

Her focus was so intense it made the swords look slow—as if the world was usually on fast-forward. And the fear radar was working—the same one she'd tried without success earlier in the day.

Not only was it working, it was far more effective than Dread's.

Her grasp of impending threats was as vivid as if they had already happened.

Pushed beyond her limits, Sally had awakened and was hurtling toward new heights.

"I can't hit her! Dammit!"

"I won't lose. Not here...!"

Every swing Sally took landed. Every swing aimed at her missed.

She used Attack Lure again and again, and by the time Frederica started to sense something was amiss, Sally had already slain twenty players.

"It's...*not* a skill?!" Frederica gasped, finally grasping the truth.

But that meant...there was *nothing* they could do.

Their countermeasures were useless. This horrifying realization began to spread through the crowd.

Unfortunately, knowing didn't help.

"Rah!"

As a powerful blow hurtled toward her, Sally stepped out of the way—

However, she didn't *just* dodge.

She evaded it by a hairbreadth and immediately landed a counter.

"Now!"

Spells shot toward her, but she'd instinctively guessed the timing of their attack.

"Shoulder Throw!"

She sheathed her weapons, grabbed a player, and promptly threw them into the air.

The player's body blocked the incoming spells, and not one of them reached Sally.

Since friendly fire was off, their ally took no damage, but on the way down, Sally mercilessly laid into them.

"Is she even human...?"

They still had seventy players—but put another way, they'd already lost thirty. The fact that the outcome of this battle was even in question proved Sally had already broken their spirit, all on her own.

"Oboro, Shadow Clone."

This was no time to keep tricks up her sleeve.

Sally's survival depended on constant surprises and keeping her foes second-guessing themselves.

"I'm gonna survive...and take you all out!"

Unlike the real Sally, her clones were soon taken out. But each took at least one foe down with them.

And Sally herself was trying to break out of the center.

But then—

"Gotcha!"
A sword stabbed her in the back.
A cheer went up from the crowd.
"Nope, not yet."
The Mirage-generated fake dissolved.
There was no end to the shocking surprises.
Frederica had started out confidently barking orders from the back, but Sally was too great a threat for that—she was now in the fray herself.
If Sally hadn't limit broken herself, she'd have been dead long ago.
Surrounding Sally forced her to confront her own limits—defeating her required they prevent Sally from surpassing them.
"Multi-Firebolt!"
Frederica was watching Sally with disbelief.
Literally nothing had hit her yet.
They were missing by a fraction of an inch—but that tiny distance seemed insurmountable.
"We're in trouble…!"
Since Sally was prioritizing survival, she wasn't eliminating players very quickly, but she was still taking out a *lot*.
Frederica had chosen a location with plenty of cover as it was the ideal place to set up an ambush. But now the terrain was helping Sally stay alive.

"*Tsk…* More enemies catching up?"
Members of other guilds were chasing down the orbs she held,

joining the encirclement. Even as she realized this, Sally had to keep moving, dodging Frederica's bombardment.

"I'm good. I can still do...this?"

Out of nowhere—

Her feet stopped. She fell to her knees.

"Water Wall!"

She managed to roll out of the path of the oncoming firebolts, but a moment later, she was surrounded.

This was a group of very cautious players. Wary of some new trick, they did not immediately attack.

She'd already pulled tricks like that repeatedly.

But she'd also been moving beyond her limits for some time now.

That wasn't something anyone could keep up for long.

Frederica placed barriers on everyone. Watching them step closer, Sally whispered, "You won't get me twice."

"Multi-Firebolt."

At Frederica's chant—everything exploded.

But it wasn't because of Frederica's spell.

Flames arced through the sky, trailing smoke—like a meteor hurtling toward them.

It landed between Frederica and Sally.

And then the glare of the firebolts blinded everyone.

When the dazzle died down, a girl with white wings and black armor stood before them.

"You can't have her," Maple said. "Not on my watch."

Maple summoned Syrup, barking an order.

"Rampart!"

Walls rose out of the ground, obscuring Sally and Maple from view.

The barriers towered so high Frederica's team could not hope to scale them.

"Maple...how...?"

It was too great a distance for her to have ridden Syrup.

Sally had known she'd never make it in time—that was why she hadn't asked for help.

"I'll explain later! I left Mai and Yui on their own, so we gotta head back quick! Grab hold!"

"O-okay..." Sally forced herself to her feet and put her arms around Maple.

Maple secured Sally, holding her tight, and got ready to make their escape.

"Deploy Artillery."

Weapons sprouted from every inch of Maple, filling the interior of the ramparts.

And every barrel was pointed down.

"Here we go!"

"What?! Y-you've gotta be kidding me!"

Heedless of Sally's panic, every weapon fired, belching fire and smoke.

It was basically self-destruct.

But Maple could soak all the damage.

Scrapping her top-tier weapons in the ensuing explosion, she launched herself into the skies above.

Without the leg stabilizers, the recoil would send her flying. That much force would normally kill any player. But since Maple was immune to it, the move turned her into a rocket.

When she reached the peak of her trajectory, she started shouting skill names.

"Full Deploy! Commence Assault! Hydra!"

Laser after laser fired at the ground below. Like an endless meteor shower, hundreds of shots gouged the earth, scorching the players unlucky enough to get hit.

And these were followed by a three-headed dragon that turned the area into a lake of poison.

Few people with Frederica had Poison Nullification. They hadn't planned on fighting Maple, so most hadn't equipped their anti-Maple gear.

They proved no match for Hydra.

Just as they had Sally cornered, they were sent back to their guild, not even sure what had happened.

Sally had killed thirty.

And Maple had killed far more than that.

Had it not been for that carpet-bombing from above, they surely wouldn't have lost that many.

"That's for going after Sally!"

With another blast of flame, she flew back toward the Maple Tree base.

"Ughh... What *was* thaaat?!"

Frederica had thrown out every defense she had, and she had Poison Nullification, so she'd managed to survive. Barely. Sitting in a lake of poison.

"We're not letting you get away scot-free...!"

She was in shambles, her ploy completely foiled, but she had one bright idea left.

One that might make up for this unmitigated disaster.

If it didn't pay off, Pain could complain all he liked, and she wouldn't be able to object.

"Please, Dread! Do something..."

He wasn't even here to hear her plea, but she had to pin her prayers on him.

Mai and Yui were standing before the orbs.

"Do you think Maple made it in time?"

"She and Sally were together on my map, so I think she did!"

"How'd she get there so fast?"

"I dunno. But she said she'd be back soon!"

But they weren't sure how soon that would be.

"Yui, I made sure we were ready."

"Good. But...are you sure we shouldn't wake Kanade and Chrome? It *would* be safer..."

They decided to play it safe...

But they weren't given time.

"! Yui! It's the enemy!"

"Huh?!"

The twins raised their hammers.

A single player was walking into the entrance.

Dread.

They'd located Maple Tree's base.

The Order of the Holy Sword hadn't tried anything, because Maple was too dangerous. But with her gone and Dread lying in wait nearby—why *wouldn't* he attack?

"*Sigh*...Frederica sure knows how to work a man to the bone. Are we sure Maple's not here? If she really is gone...I got this."

He'd headed straight in the moment he got Frederica's message.

It would only be a matter of minutes before Maple got back, but that was a long time for Mai and Yui to hold out.

"Yui, we're taking him down!"

"I know!"

They both popped a Doping Seed, boosting their STR still further.

They couldn't afford to lose here.

"Ha...not happening." Dread broke into a dead run, drawing closer with every second.

Yui swung her hammer down.

He was still a decent distance away, but that didn't matter.

"Farshot!"

The skill made her hammer glow, and a shock wave shot out— one guaranteed to be fatal.

"Hmph!"

But Dread dodged it.

He did it without even slowing down.

"Double Stamp!"

As he dodged Yui's attack, Dread targeted Mai, swinging his dagger.

"Mai!"

"I-I'm okay!"

It was pure chance she managed to dodge his blow.

He used the same weapon as Sally, and she could recognize that attack motion anywhere. Her body had instinctively started moving before her conscious mind even realized it.

But that wouldn't happen twice.

Dread had received a full briefing on the twins' raw DPS output from scout units.

As a result, he was being careful not to get hit and avoiding getting too close. That was what had allowed Mai to survive.

"Mai! Get back a little!"

"Okay!"

Mai ran toward the wall.

But Dread was far faster. He caught up quick.

"You're slow."

"……! Augh!!"

Dread's dagger swung toward her.

But then— Mai threw her weapon at Dread.

"Huh?!"

He hadn't expected this desperate strategy.

Seeing his surprise, Mai grinned. "That won't hit!"

Again, his body contorted out of the weapon's path. Now Mai was unarmed. His blade swung toward her again—until a shudder made him leap backward.

An instant later, a shock wave erupted where he'd just been standing.

"The other one…! What?"

He'd turned to see the glow of a skill about to activate—on Yui's *second* hammer.

The one Mai had thrown.

"Crap…gah?!"

The second shock wave hit him hard, slamming him into the wall.

Mai hadn't been armed with a hammer. She'd merely been holding the hammer Yui had equipped.

When she'd thrown it, she'd just been giving it back.

Once it was back in her hands, Yui could activate a second—unexpected—skill.

This was one hell of a trick that only the two of them could pull off.

"We're barely half a player on our own—"

"But if we join forces—"

""We can beat *any* player.""

They might still be lacking in experience and technique, but this was a big step toward true greatness.

A very big step.

But not far enough.

"Damn, you're *all* brutal."

""No way?!""

"One down!"

Dread's dagger tore Mai open.

She had no way of withstanding this.

Dread's HP had exactly one point remaining. That wasn't luck. It was clearly the work of a skill.

This was the advantage of time.

He'd just been playing that much longer than them.

"Bye...!"

"Maple...sorry..."

He'd turned the tables on their secret plan, and his blades took Yui down in short order.

Dread sheathed his daggers and chugged a potion, restoring his HP.

"*Sigh*...what a mess. This whole guild's a headache."

When his HP was topped up, he turned toward their orb, muttering, "Looks like I win this time— Huh?!"

Time ran out before he touched the orb.

There was an explosive roar behind him. Maple had brought Sally back.

"......I'll have to make it up to the twins later."

"Fredericaaaa! You owe me one!"

Dread had won the match but lost the battle.

The twins had bought enough time.

And Maple wasn't about to waste this opportunity.

CHAPTER 4

Defense Build and the Unleashing

On their way back to the base, Maple consulted Sally on an important detail—which abilities she could reveal for day two. She had a particular one in mind—a versatile, cost-efficient skill.

And when she found Dread waiting for her, she went right for it.

"Predators!"

Two hideous monsters emerged from the ground.

This was the first time she'd used them in public, and Dread was *not* prepared.

"The hell is that?!"

"Syrup! Mother Nature!"

At her command, vines snaked out of the ground, surrounding Dread and Maple, sealing them all inside.

The walls kept weaving tighter, the space shrinking.

Dread slashed the barrier, trying to break out, but quickly realized that would take far too long.

He abandoned the idea, focusing on Maple herself.

"...Okay, my loss. Next time, I'll be prepped and ready for ya."

He'd only just finished fighting the twins and had not been expecting Maple to arrive in time to catch him.

But she had, and now she had him trapped.

It was chance that had given her this advantage, but next time…

Well, under any other circumstances, he could at least run away.

"And I'll just kill you again!" Maple shouted.

Her Predators launched themselves toward him.

"Oh, next time it'll be a Maple hunt!"

And with that, Dread turned to light.

Maple couldn't miss the vicious grin on his face. That was the smirk of a man with a plan.

She had Syrup cancel Mother Nature and went back to Sally.

The skill had successfully kept her out of the fight.

Maple made a beeline for her and pinched her cheeks.

"You're such a tryhard!"

"…Sorry."

"Save that for the twins when they respawn."

"Will do."

Before long, Mai and Yui showed back up.

Maple and Sally immediately apologized, but the twins weren't the least bit upset. In fact, they seemed quite proud of themselves for having held off a powerful foe long enough for Maple to get back.

"Better put these orbs out," Sally said, and ten orbs rolled out of her inventory.

"Sally, why would you push yourself like this? You could have swung back home earlier!"

"Yeah, about that…uh, better get Kanade out here first."

"It's almost time to change shifts. I'll go get him!"

Mai dashed down the hall and came back with Kanade in tow.

"Kanade, hate to rush you, but stick this in your brain."

Sally showed him her map.

"Wow...," he murmured in wonder.

Everyone leaned in and saw nearly every inch of the event's map bursting with intel.

She'd spent twelve straight hours running and had filled her map with guild positions, sizes, and more.

"I'm...really past my limit. Kanade, make sure you put this all on Maple's map."

"Mm, got it. It's all up here," he said, tapping his head. His memory was superhuman and could retain all that info at a glance.

"Thanks. Maple, time for Plan B."

They'd come up with this in case the front line collapsed.

But once the event was actually underway, things hadn't all gone the way Sally thought; she'd decided it was best to change tack.

Plan B.

Aka: Unleash the Maple.

Freed from the shackles of guard duty, their greatest weapon would be running amok outside.

Sally's info had given them nearly every guild's location. Now they just had to send in the real monster.

"Call me if the defense is in trouble—I'll fly right home!"

"Is there a cap on that?" Sally asked.

Maple did some quick math.

"Depends on the distance, but—uh, how far did I fly to save you? I can manage that round trip twice a day, I think."

Her flight was powered by weapon destruction, so it wasn't *always* available.

And if she burned those to take flight, she couldn't use them to attack.

Best to use it sparingly.

"I'll start from the outside and work my way in, then fly the last stretch home."

With Sally's map, she didn't need to waste time searching. Maple could just plot the most efficient route.

That saved a lot of time.

"I'll just...rest awhile."

"Yep, I'm tagging in."

As Sally left the ring, Maple entered.

Everything was in place.

"I'll head out at first light!"

"And I'll put this all on your map before you go."

Kanade quickly started scribbling.

The next morning...

One midsize guild breathed a sigh of relief. They'd made it to dawn.

"*Whew*...finally, some light!"

"No more night raids! Life will be so much easier!"

"...Enemy incoming! They're solo!"

Their early morning peace was instantly shattered.

Tensing themselves, all eyes turned toward this lone invader.

A girl in black armor walked straight into their base, not even bothering to hide.

The incarnation of broken. The symbol of death. The embodiment of madness.

The one player who didn't *need* to defend herself—

Maple.

*　　*　　*

"L-let's do this! Protect the orb!"

""""Urahhh!""""

But even as they braced themselves...Maple was getting ready to go all out.

"Predators!"

The one new attack they were letting her reveal.

One strong enough to shatter the spirits of any other player.

Ripping players apart, the creatures she summoned advanced relentlessly.

Unbridled violence, inexorably driven home.

They knew where she was, how she was attacking, even had a general idea of her stats—but none of that helped them stop her.

Maple walked in lockstep with death incarnate.

Not a glimmer of hope was left in her wake.

Any guild she targeted—was doomed.

Maple had left at daybreak. Until then, she'd stayed put at the base.

She couldn't risk leaving until Sally's ten-orb haul was scored.

Sally was sleeping like the dead in back—it did not seem like she'd be up for a while. Kanade had transferred her map data to everybody else. And there was no need to gather repair items—they had Iz.

Which left them with no real reason to leave the base.

While only a few foes were likely to attack Maple Tree *because* Maple was absent, they definitely needed a group on guard.

"So? Do we wanna send anyone else out? Just...thinning the enemy ranks?" Chrome suggested.

"Hmm. I can do that," Kasumi volunteered. "Iz's bombs and the twins' throws can deal plenty of damage, and you're enough defense all on your own."

She headed toward the exit.

"Don't take any crazy risks."

"Yeah, I'll make sure to stay alive."

And with that, she vanished down the passage.

Kasumi had spent the bulk of the first day teamed with Iz.

Their peculiar tactics had required specific base layouts, so they'd mostly spent time eliminating the competition.

With Iz around, she never had to worry about her equipment's durability, so they'd spent the night throwing themselves at any players they ran across.

Even without Maple, fighting Maple Tree was a harrowing endeavor.

And players who'd died once would avoid attacking any Maple Tree members afterward.

Their home base was also getting attacked less because Kasumi and Iz had steadily added to the death count of all the players in the vicinity.

This tactic was the epitome of slow and steady, and it was highly effective.

That's why Kasumi planned to spend the second day doing the exact same thing.

"Best if I go the opposite direction from Maple."

It was futile to expect Maple to leave survivors in her wake.

"Let's try this way." Kasumi picked a forest that offered lots of places to hide.

She'd been spending a lot of time in rough terrain like this. The ample cover not only kept her hidden—it encouraged other players to patrol the area, giving her plenty of targets.

"Speak of the devil."

Spotting a player, she swiftly attacked from behind.

"You should be more vigilant," she suggested.

Sparks flying, they spun around, wildly flailing with their sword, hoping to connect.

But Kasumi deflected this clumsy attempt easily, attacking again—all movements she'd done countless times before, and they proved their usefulness once again.

She quickly killed three players in the forest, checked her katana's durability, then set off once more.

"I'll have to ask Iz to repair it when I get back."

Just as she left the forest, she ran into a male player.

".........Oh! I know you!"

"...I was just leaving," Kasumi said, grimacing.

But this guy wasn't letting her go.

"Man, I was totally planning on inviting you to our guild and everything."

"Sorry, but Maple beat you to it."

Every guild was on the lookout for talent.

Maple Tree was hardly the only guild that had been after top players like Kasumi and Chrome.

The man facing her shrugged her dismissive comment off, then locked eyes with her.

"You got me in the first event," he admitted. "But not this time."

He drew his one-handed sword and raised his shield.

This was Shin—the man known on the server as Splinter Sword. He and Kasumi had fought each other in the first event, and she'd emerged victorious.

"*Sigh...* Enjoy your respawn!" Kasumi said, drawing her katana.

Shin hadn't earned his nickname for nothing.

"Splinter Sword!" he yelled—and his sword fell apart, leaving the resulting pieces to float in the air.

They formed ten blades, each like a miniature version of the original.

A shield on one arm. Ten blades in the air around him.

Manipulating these flying blades was how Shin fought—and Kasumi knew full well how long his range was. She wouldn't be getting away easily.

"Hah!"

His blades shot toward her.

"Hmph!"

With a quick grunt, she knocked as many down as she could—or deflected them—focusing on defense.

Kasumi couldn't dodge like Sally did. She was steadily taking damage.

But she could tank that. Unlike Sally, she had plenty of HP.

Avoiding any blades aimed at her torso, she kept fighting.

"First Blade: Heat Haze!"

This helped her close instantly with Shin, letting her slash at him.

But he blocked the attack with his shield.

"Yep, still one heck of a skill! Can't survive it without a shield."

"Hah...I've had someone stone-cold dodge it!"

The skill motion completed, she attacked again.

This, too, was blocked; and Kasumi sensed the blades coming in from behind. She was forced to retreat.

Having fought before, they both had a sense of the other's style; neither was catching the other by surprise or able to land a decisive blow.

But it had been a while since the first event.

And neither had been slacking off. They'd both found ways to improve.

The one who could weather the other's improved arsenal would decide the outcome.

Kasumi was biding her time, waiting for the chance to go on the offensive.

Shin had a shield, which meant it was possible he could even block the move she'd used on Sally—Final Blade: Misty Moon.

Once she used that skill, Kasumi would take a huge stat hit and lose access to some of her skills to boot.

But it was as powerful as it was swift.

An ultimate move only useful one-on-one.

If it wasn't for Shin's shield, she'd have used it already.

"Hah......! Hngg!"

She spun, her katana lashing out, escaping the flying swords.

Those gave him a reach advantage, preventing her from getting in close.

And on top of that, he'd gotten a lot better at precision control.

Feeling like he was going to win the battle of attrition, she decided to force an opportunity.

"Fourth Blade: Whirlwind."

A high-speed four-hit combo. Shin caught each blow on his shield.

Then the flying swords came in, digging into her HP. Still, she endured.

Splinter Sword sacrificed the power of each individual blow in exchange for a much higher quantity of hits.

It would take all those blades scoring clean hits to down Kasumi.

"Seventh Blade: Pulverize."

This was a strong blow from above with a knockback effect.

Shin caught it, sliding away.

The true value of this skill was the massive amount of damage it did to equipment.

Naturally, it did far more damage to her opponent's, but the damage to her own blade was nothing to sneeze at.

In other words, Kasumi had decided her best path to victory was to break Shin's shield before her HP ran out.

"You've raised your STR...more than I expected!"

He commanded his blades to swing back around between them, stopping her advance.

And...

"Splinter Sword!"

A second activation.

Shin's true power was one unknown to Kasumi.

The blades grew smaller still, splitting into twenty shards. Then he sent them all head-on toward her.

She hadn't expected a veritable wall of blades to come after her, and a lot of them connected with her body. Each strike did little damage, but they gave her no time to recover. Her HP was at its limit.

"...No other way, I guess," Kasumi whispered. She went limp.

"I told you I'd win this time!"

Once again, the tiny blades shot toward her.

"Origin Blade: Void."

Kasumi's hair turned white, and her eyes shone with a scarlet light.

Shin took one look and instinctively braced himself. She'd been in this state last time, too. The time he'd lost.

And right before his very eyes—Kasumi vanished.

"......! Where—?!"

"Here."

The voice came from right behind him.

Before he could turn around, two arms grew from his chest. More accurately, Kasumi's hands impaled him from behind.

"...Damn. I lose again?"

Shin shattered, turning to light.

"...No. It's a tie...or my loss, really," Kasumi muttered.

Like Final Blade, this skill had a steep penalty. Not to her stats— This one affected her equipment durability.

Barely hanging on to begin with, her gear was unable to survive the hit. Everything except her accessories disappeared. Including her katana.

"Didn't expect this much to break. Guess I've been cutting it too close."

If she encountered anyone else bereft of her mainstay weapons and armor, she was in serious trouble.

She quickly equipped her backup weapon, activated Superspeed, and raced back to their base.

"Ugh...I liked that one, too."

She keenly felt the loss of her favorite sword.

This fortunately only lasted approximately five minutes, ending when she got back to the guild and Iz agreed to reforge the blade.

As Kasumi and Shin wrapped up their duel, Maple was busy being a walking natural disaster.

"Next...is that way!"

She was already tired of walking and hopped on Syrup's back so she could fly.

This naturally drew a *lot* of attention.

As she drew near the next guild, she could hear screams from the ground below.

"Acid Rain!"

Poison began gushing down, tormenting the players below.

"Let it rain, let it rain, let it rain!" Maple sang.

She kept the deluge going a bit, then noticed there were far fewer players than before and hopped down.

"Predators!"

The survivors were already hurting, and the monsters made short work of them.

"Mwa-ha-ha…and now your orb is mine!"

She checked her map, picked her next target, and left the ruined guild behind.

"Hmm, I'd love to switch to Atrocity and run, but I can't. If only I could borrow Sally's feet!"

That was not currently a thing she could do.

At best, she could have Sally carry her.

But with Sally still in bed, there was no telling when that courier service would become available.

"I guess Syrup is my best option."

Maple was not one to worry about how much attention she was drawing. She kept right on turtle-riding.

"Hmm, nobody's coming after me. But Sally had so many people chasing her around!"

The main difference was that Sally had stolen her orbs, while Maple was simply murdering everyone first.

Nobody was stupid enough to bother chasing after her. Even after she'd taken out six whole guilds.

"I'm getting these orbs faster than Sally thought I would! This is easy."

Maple sprawled out on Syrup's back...until she heard swords clashing below.

She pulled herself to the edge of Syrup's shell and peered down. Several players were fighting over orbs below.

One guild had lost their orb to a powerful opponent, and its members were rushing out to get it back.

"Why are they all fighting? Oh! That orb's the one I wanted next!"

After seeing an orb already in the middle of a maelstrom of swords and sorcery, moving on to the next target would be prudent.

Sally would have done so.

However, Maple moved directly over the orb, and without a second's hesitation, jumped right down.

Truly death from above. She and her pet monsters entered the eye of the storm.

"That orb's mine!"

This was not true.

But there were strong odds it soon would be.

"Hydra!"

She aimed her deluge of poison directly downward, and the noxious liquid splashed off the ground, spraying in every direction.

It was almost like a fountain of powerful poison centered on Maple herself. Anyone unlucky enough to be in proximity was swiftly swallowed up. And with the ground covered in poison, no one could get anywhere near her.

One of Maple's great strengths was her tendency to use tactics so mind-boggling that nobody could react in time.

But when she turned toward the pedestal, the orb was already gone.

A quick-witted player had spotted an opportunity and nabbed the prize first.

And she had no idea who.

"Huh? What now…? Oh! Syrup, Mother Nature!"

She was in a flat area with scattered trees, and she hastily grew some vines, encircling the crowd.

Maple looked around, assuming the orb thief hadn't gone far and was hopefully trapped in her vine prison.

"Sally's notes say: 'If you can't catch 'em, kill 'em all!' That's what I'll do!"

There was no easy way to tell who held the orb, but if everyone died, it was bound to drop eventually.

Killing players on this scale was hardly easy—unless you were Maple and amply motivated.

But she was still shackled by restraint, which prevented her from using most of her moves. So she simply expanded the lake of poison, reducing the area her enemies could stand safely and penning them in like cattle.

The players had abandoned their battle and were working together, hell-bent on survival. Maple was too slow to catch up with any of them.

"Hngg, it's not working! Syrup!" Maple ordered her pet to generate more vines, with herself at the center.

She was soon dangling from a sphere of plants that reached into the sky above her vine prison.

"Deploy Artillery!"

Weapons spawned all over her. This was the same move she'd used to save Sally.

But this time she was being even more thorough.

"Commence Assault!"

A barrage of laser fire rained down on players and forced them to make evasive maneuvers in the increasingly limited terrain outside the poison lake. Nobody here was capable of succeeding.

One after another, they were swallowed up by the threat from above.

The poison lake had seemed like a failed strategy only moments earlier, but it was paying off big-time.

"I guess I can go down now," Maple said.

She landed and started looking for survivors. Instead, she found the orb sitting in a pool of her poison.

"Oh! I got 'em! Nice."

She scooped up the prize, lowered the prison walls, and flew away on Syrup's back.

"I might have to start conserving Hydra soon...but I don't wanna reveal my machine form yet, and if I have to do that again... Hmm..."

The sun on the second day had yet to reach its zenith.

Like Sally, Maple couldn't spend all day out wreaking havoc, but for very different reasons.

"Maybe one...or two more? Yeah, let's go with that." She quickly picked out her targets. Once those were done, she'd head on home.

The Maple Tree members on guard duty had nothing to do.

Currently, they only had their own orb to look after, so nobody was coming to get theirs back.

Sally was still out like a light, and Iz was busy forging Kasumi's new katana.

Kasumi was pacing back and forth behind her, fretting about her blade.

This would have been the ideal moment to raid their base, but the first day had sealed their reputation, and nobody even wanted to risk reconnoitering them.

Once Maple was unleashed, the spectators all began talking about her threat level.

"What is she even *doing*?!"

"Argh... You take your eyes off her for one minute and she gets even worse!"

They were well aware they might all have to face her someday and would not stand a chance. How could they do anything but laugh?

"She's got more than poison now...and what are those cannons?! Or the wings?!"

"Why are there lasers in a game with archers?!"

"Forget that, what are those...*things* with her? They look like they've crawled out of the bowels of hell!"

"Aughhhh, if I run into her again, I'm *so* dead! Can't you evolve on more of a...gentle slope? You're gonna give us a heart attack, Maple!"

The danger she posed had clearly more than doubled since the last event.

"She looks so adorable with her angel wings, but she's flanked by hideous horrors! You don't *need* those things! Maple, please!"

And even as they talked, players who'd been eliminated by her rampage started showing up and sharing their tales. Everyone was hungry for details, hoping for even a glimpse at a survival strategy.

"Hard to tell what the angel thing is all about from just a video feed, but those nobly sacrificed to her exploits claim she's soaking damage for everyone else in her party. I guess it's like an AOE Cover? That's what I heard, at least."

"She's no angel, then. Lord...a perpetual Maple cover?!"

"That's hell on earth! At least it looks pretty."

"Who even stands a chance against it? You're better off running for the hills. Avoid anyone strong! Only way to stay alive."

"But with the orbs…that's not a viable strategy."

"Oh, Maple's definitely got the spotlight, but those two kids with the giant hammers? They're pretty nuts in their own right."

"Lots of people claiming those girls one-shot them."

"Does their guild have *zero* normal members? Is it all top rankers or monsters?"

"They're placed fifth right now! You can't get your orb back without taking Maple out, so that's not happening. Nobody's even trying anymore."

"High risk, low return… Scratch that. Let's just say 'no return.'"

"They're gonna have to face the Order or Flame Empire eventually, right? So many guilds getting eliminated. The big guilds still hold the lead for now…"

The audience found it hard to believe anyone could take the two biggest guilds that stood at the top.

"Well, not like the feed's showing everything that's happening. But if anyone's fighting Maple, I wanna watch."

And as they talked, more eliminated players arrived, sharing stories about the titans who'd defeated them.

CHAPTER 5

Defense Build and Best-Laid Plans

Just past noon on the event's second day...

Sally slowly sat up in the back passage of the Maple Tree base.

"...How's she doing?" she muttered, opening her map to check Maple's location.

The icon's movements suggested she was on her way back home.

"Time I got going, then."

As a result of her ultra-focused forced march, Sally was still not feeling like herself, but she couldn't exactly sleep all day.

Sally heaved herself to her feet and headed into the orb chamber.

As she joined the defensive line, she saw their own orb on the pedestal.

She looked relieved, stretched, and joined the other guild members.

"Oh, you're up!" Chrome said. "What's the plan? You headed out again?"

Sally shook her head. She was still feeling off her game and wasn't sure she'd be able to evade properly.

It was the second day now, so surviving guilds were going to be far better at reacting to surprise attacks. And if the element of surprise failed Sally, she was dead. Consequently, she'd decided to stick to the base until dark.

She brought up the elephant in the room.

"What's up with Kasumi...?"

"Yeah, uh...she's been like that since she got her new katana."

They both watched her for a while.

Nobody had ever seen her smiling this much. She stared in absolute rapture at her scabbard, then blissfully at her blade, then back again.

"Ahhhhh...perfection..."

She seemed unlikely to come back to reality any time soon.

"Sounds like she took out Splinter Sword. Wonder how many top-class players'll die as we head into the back half of the event..."

"The last day will be pure chaos. They'll likely all still be up and kicking."

Dread and Shin had both died because they'd gone up against other top players.

But as long as the powerful avoided one another, they wouldn't die easy.

At this point, Maple strolled back in.

"I'm back! With nine new orbs!"

"Holy—you don't play around, huh?"

Maple had brought back almost as many orbs as Sally had without looking any worse for wear.

"Only because I had your map, Sally. Otherwise I'd have been searching blind..."

"Glad to be of service!"

Maple dumped all her orbs on the pedestal and prudently chose to stay within the base.

Her skill uses were running low, and while odds were slim,

there was still a chance all these guilds she'd attacked would show up to try and get their orbs back.

Not that many players were willing to charge blindly into almost certain death, but better safe than sorry.

"Also, from what I could see while flying around, there's a *lot* of fighting going on. I bet there's a bunch of people racking up deaths."

"We've already reached that point, huh?" Chrome said. "Everyone's given up on getting orbs back from the big guilds, so their only option is to fight one another."

"Sounds about right. So nice of them to take each other out."

Players like Sally had spent the first day forcing everyone to the brink, and it was hard to fight against that feeling of desperation.

If anything, it was getting stronger.

"Mai and Yui are real good at defense, and this cave has been a huge help."

Currently, the twins were playing catch. With an iron sphere.

Neither were quick on their feet or great when heavily outnumbered. In this event format, they were unlikely to be very useful out in the field. That meant they were more or less permanently stuck on guard duty. Unfortunately, when nobody was attacking, having nothing to do got old fast.

"Once these orbs are scored, let's give them a chance to strut their stuff."

"Mm? Sally, aren't they already doing that?"

"Oh, I mean…outside."

Chrome frowned, but before he could say anything about mobility, Sally grabbed Maple's ear.

"Maple, you making another run's not an option, right?"

She was asking how many skill uses Maple had left.

Sally might have been asleep all morning, but she had a good idea how much Maple had burned through—they'd spent enough time together.

"Mm...yeah, I'd better not. Oh! You mean—?"

"Exactly. If you take them with you, you won't have to do it all yourself. Doesn't seem like we've really gotta worry about defending this place anyway."

And Maple could rocket back here if the need ever arose.

She was the linchpin of their defense *and* their offense.

"All right, then once we're done guarding this pile, I'll take the twins out to play."

"Just lemme know if it's too much, okay?"

Sally had run herself ragged and didn't want to force that on anyone else.

"The second event toughened me up! And it's not like I've been walking anywhere."

There was no use in Maple trying to run around on foot like Sally did, and riding her turtle around was actually quite relaxing.

"In that case, take it away."

"You got it!"

Three hours later, Maple set out once again with two of the most destructive beings on the server. Though she was nigh invincible, her main weakness was her relatively low DPS, especially if a fight dragged on. That wasn't a problem if she was with the attack specialists, Mai and Yui—especially since Maple more than made up for their lack of defense.

When the three of them joined forces, their horrendously unbalanced builds worked in perfect unison, making them a nightmare for anyone unlucky enough to run into them.

As the afternoon on the second day began, it was pretty clear who stood a chance at finishing on top.

Maple Tree, Flame Empire, and the Order of the Holy Sword were way ahead of the competition.

The two biggest guilds—and a tiny one. Everyone was acutely aware of how strange this was.

Flame Empire was definitely concerned about them.

Scouts had brought back reports that Maple was on the prowl, and Marx had been busy changing up his traps, trying to strategize against her.

"But…it's *Maple*…so let's just hope she doesn't come here."

"I know, right?" Misery said. "Fingers crossed. Shin already died once, so I pray they keep their distance."

Neither the Trapper nor the Saint had builds that were much use against Maple.

And without an effective strategy, it would be hard for them to last long.

Shin had headed back out into the field, undaunted.

Mii was out, too.

But even as the defense leaders spoke, a frantic player came running their way.

"Marx! There's a turtle flying this way!"

"Eep. Oh no…"

"Okay. Now what?"

They'd only ever heard of one flying turtle.

The last foe they wanted to meet, the infamous code red…was inbound.

"Misery…call Mii back."

"Yeah, we'd better."

"I'll do my best to buy time. I should be able to— Well, let's hope I can."

"No use standing here."

They rounded up everyone with piercing skills and got ready to meet the approaching turtle.

When they reached the front lines, they saw the shadow slowly flying their way.

As they watched, it grew steadily larger.

"Any word from Mii?"

"Headed our way."

"Got it. I think I can last ten minutes, but more than that…"

If Mii wasn't here by then, odds were their defenses would crumble.

"I'll back you up as best I can."

"Thanks. First, let's bring her to ground level. Archers and mages, ready!"

But even as they braced themselves, the turtle vanished just outside their range.

Three silhouettes fell toward the ground.

All three moved *very* slowly. None of them looked remotely normal.

On the first figure's back were a pair of beautiful white wings, and at her sides were two hideous abominations.

The other two players each carried a pair of hammers—a feat that by all accounts should have been impossible. The sheer size of the weapons in their tiny hands alone sent shock rippling through the crowd.

Marx had wanted them on the ground…but if they'd simply flown directly at them, it would have been a lot less intimidating.

"You can do it. You just have to buy time!"

He never even considered winning.

He just had to hold the line.

He knew full well that was his only option.

Maple came walking straight in, and the traps Marx had prepared went off one after another.

Unfortunately, they didn't do anything.

There was no doubt they activated properly. Maple's defense was just so high they didn't even faze her.

"Yeah… That's what I was afraid of…"

Traps that could have easily killed dozens had all gone to waste. Marx threw his hands up in resignation.

But he'd also prepared some special traps just for her arrival.

"Got her…!"

As Maple stepped on one of these, a slew of plants started growing. The stems and vines coiled around her arms and legs, preventing her from moving.

These blockers were pretty good against low-Agility players like her.

You had to do a fair bit of damage to them to break free, but with her limbs trapped, Maple couldn't use her weapon. Based on how his own skills worked, Marx had correctly deduced that most of Maple's big moves had a hard use limit.

He'd figured she wouldn't want to throw those around with wild abandon, and even if she did bust one out, that would be one less threat Mii would have to deal with.

Marx was fully expecting to die before this was over, so if he could force Maple to use up a big skill, that was all part of the plan.

"Huh…?"

His plan had not accounted for Mai and Yui turning his plants into a pile of kindling. With a single strike at that.

"Uh, are you for real?"

Traps kept going off. Maple soaked up all the damage while the twins freed her from the bonds, and they just kept coming. Completely unscathed.

"Misery!"

"On it!"

She started barking orders, and a barrage of spells with piercing effects hurtled toward the Maple Tree spearhead.

Long-distance spells didn't usually deal lethal damage.

But they could force people to take evasive action. And that helped buy time.

Maple's group wasn't making good progress.

They kept dodging into trap after trap. The biggest delays came when the piercing attacks and restraining traps overlapped.

This would be much easier if Maple could free herself from those.

"Right, Sally had a tip for this!"

She took a deep breath and then yelled a skill name—loud enough that her enemy could hear. "Weapon Enlargement!" Then she said a real skill under her breath. "Deploy Bayonet."

Metal covered her weapon hand, forming a blade as long as she was tall.

Another one of Sally's tricks.

She'd suggested hiding the true nature of Machine God, using pieces of it if needed, but keeping anyone from guessing that all her deployments were parts of the same thing.

The sword made her arm heavy, but the skill bonus kept it relatively mobile. Maple pressed the blade against the plants pinning it in place, snapped them in two, then swung around, cutting her feet free.

Marx was likely tearing his hair out by this point.

"Come on!" Maple said.

""Okay!""

Every step she took sprung another trap. Walls rose up, pits reared open from beneath, and spells rained down from above.

But nothing stopped them.

Mai and Yui were too powerful for any obstacles to hold them, and the traps Marx had been certain would slow Maple down... didn't.

"Right, then. Everyone, pull back."

Marx sent everyone but Misery to the base proper.

"Certain death, then?" she said.

"You got it."

Once Maple Tree cleared the traps, they'd have to face Flame Empire's top defenders...

The Trapper and the Saint.

These two were the last line of defense and the only players present who had a shot at handling this threat. They were both primarily spellcasters. And they'd figured out the angel wings and her zone of defense. They were focused on piercing attacks from outside that range—

—because inside the glowing circle, the twins were free to do as they pleased. Stepping in there with them was extremely dangerous.

And with all the traps on this field, Mai and Yui weren't able to take a step beyond the reach of Maple's skill.

To recover the HP she'd lost, Maple left attacking up to them, while she used her Meditation skill.

""Farshot!""

Mai and Yui had ranged attacks that packed lethal force.

But at this distance, they were uselessly inaccurate.

For a while, they exchanged ranged attacks, without either side really accomplishing much.

But that standoff only lasted as long as Maple's Meditation—which had just finished.

"Hydra!"

The poison dragon attacked out of nowhere, and Marx had no time to flee.

This was an attack so powerful it consumed everything in its path.

In the battle of Maple versus Marx, it was Maple who demonstrated her true power.

Traps were his specialty, so the moment she'd thwarted those, it was clear who'd won.

"! Resurrect!"

White light shot out from Misery and wrapped around Marx.

This skill was what had earned her the Saint moniker. It only worked in the moment directly after death, but it could reverse a fatal blow.

"Remote Installation: Rock Wall! Remote Installation: Wind Blades."

As soon as Marx was alive again, he started setting new traps, running interference as best he could.

But Maple was targeting Misery now. Marx had assumed they'd hit him again, so his traps did nothing.

"Hngg…!"

Misery couldn't use Resurrect on herself.

The cost of staying alive was incredibly high.

High enough that she was better off just dying here.

Recovery magic wasn't much good against the lethal damage the twins were dishing out.

She'd made magic barriers, but their shock waves tore right through them, bearing down on her.

"Guess it's my time," Misery said, resigned to her fate.

The twins were drawing near. Too near to miss.

"Never surrender."

However, a figure blocked their advance.

It was Mii, wreathed head to toe in crimson flames.

Mii immediately used Flame Empress, followed by Detonate, the explosive blasts buffeting the advancing twins.

But since Maple was absorbing all the damage, the knockback only affected her, and this did not directly impede their progress.

But if Maple moved, so did the area her skill covered.

Now exposed, Mai and Yui couldn't risk setting off one of Marx's traps and were forced to retreat.

Mii's go-to defense approach proved remarkably effective.

"Detonate!"

"C-Cover Move!"

When Mii knocked Maple away, Yui and Mai ran back toward her while Maple warped herself closer to them.

"Mai, Yui! Over here!"

Maple called Syrup out, put the twins on its back, and sent it upward.

If Mii was gonna knock her around the field, there was a strong chance the twins would keep slipping out of her protection.

"Flame Spear! Flare Impetus!"

Mii was switching between the midrange Flame Empress and close-range attacks by conjuring a spear made of fire and setting her feet alight.

Maple swung her giant sword hand around but simply couldn't match Mii's speeds.

Her summoned Predators couldn't catch Mii, either.

"Even the Flame Empress can't?!"

Despite putting up a good fight, Mii had yet to deal any damage. She'd been hoping her strongest attack might be enough—but no dice.

"Misery! Marx!"

"Got it!"

"Yep!"

"Detonate!"

"Argh! C'mon!"

As Mii knocked Maple back, she was struck by Misery's piercing attacks.

And Marx's traps snagged her feet.

"Hngg…!"

Maple used her sword to free her feet and her shield to block the spells.

With her sword arm and great shield, she could stop most attacks from hitting.

And her Predators were such an obvious threat that the enemy fighters had to keep their distance, which meant even with Maple's speed, she could react in time.

Still, if they stayed outside the range of her monsters, that meant they were also out of reach of Maple's attacks.

She could use the skills on her short sword five times a day at no MP cost. But she only had one of those uses left and didn't want to waste it now. It would be a terrible idea to empty out her big guns.

"What should I do…? Hngg!"

Mii hit her again, and the knockback ruined her balance.

In fact, it didn't even need to hit Maple. As long as it hit her Predators, the effect knocked her back instead.

And if she landed on a trap because of it—this was a mess.

"Argh!"

Mii, Marx, and Misery were maintaining a safe distance. All three were faster than Maple, and the ground was covered in traps designed to trip her up. Three high-ranking players wouldn't fight Maple the way a monster would. This was a very frustrating strategy. None of them were foolhardy enough to attack head-on; they were smartly using their mobility advantage to search for openings.

Maple could only watch them circle her, frowning all the while.

But the Flame Empire's defenders were well aware that landing the occasional piercing blow wouldn't get them anywhere. The current situation left them with very few viable offensive options.

"Misery, I'm going for it! I'll need you to adjust our defenses after!"

"Got it!"

Mii waited for the next trap to activate, then used a skill.

"Inferno Cage!"

"Mm? Wait— Huh?!"

Flames rocketed skyward all around Maple, enclosing her in burning walls.

There was an opening above her, but it was very high up. She tried hitting the walls with her sword but failed to break through.

"Yikes, I'm taking damage?"

This cage did damage over time—damage that ignored defense. She canceled Predators and drank a potion, waiting for the skill to time out, but it seemed disinclined to do that.

This was Mii's ace in the hole—her last resort. She could only use it once a day, and the skill duration was no joke.

"What now? Hngg!"

Maple would need another plan.

Outside, Mii was emptying one MP potion after another.

Inferno Cage lasted until her MP ran out or after ten minutes passed, whichever came first. But reaching that theoretical max time forced her to down dozens of MP potions.

Given the event format, that was something she'd wanted to avoid, but against Maple, she couldn't afford to be conservative.

"Well," Mii said. "Thoughts?"

"I'm crossing my fingers this kills her."

"Yeah...I don't have many traps left in me."

But even as they spoke, Mii's flames scattered. A black mass leaped skyward, landing outside the cage.

Their collective strength had made Maple flip the forbidden switch.

"Full Deploy."

Before their very eyes, Maple transformed. Every inch of her was covered in gleaming black weaponry. An unnerving sight, to say the least.

Maple had decided she couldn't win while holding back, so she'd busted out another power.

"It's my turn to attack!"

With a clank, every weapon turned toward them.

"Commence Assault!"

"Detonate!"

Maple was firing an insane number of lasers and bullets.

Mii hastily defended, then grabbed Marx and Misery and took cover behind some trees, where Maple's attacks couldn't reach.

But if they were out of her range, then she was out of theirs.

Marx still had restraint traps out there, but those did little on their own without anyone following up with additional attacks.

"Marx, what do you think?"

"It's no use… We're doomed…"

"That's what I thought. I'm assuming that's her ultimate move, so let's call ourselves lucky we made her reveal it."

Mii made a face, then said, "Very well. We'll call it a loss, but we aren't about to go down without a fight."

She popped up her screen and sent a quick message to all guild members.

"Come."

"Okay."

With Marx and Misery in tow, Mii tried to vacate the area.

A moment later, however, there was an explosion far louder than any she'd created. They all flinched, turning toward the noise.

"Fooound you!"

Maple was right in front of them, shedding shattered guns and artillery tubes.

Before Mii could use Detonate, Maple's giant sword arm ran Misery through.

"Ack…!"

"Deploy Bayonets."

Maple's left arm generated dozens more weapons, each of them stabbing into Misery.

"Detonate!"

Mii knocked Maple away, grabbed Marx's hand, and tried to escape with Flare Impetus.

But even as the flames propelled her, Maple caught up.

Maple's self-destruct rocketed her forward. An instant later, the tip of her blade struck Marx in the back.

Like with Misery, more blades generated, piercing his arms and legs.

"Ah......!"

Marx looked down at the massive blade sticking out of his chest and slumped in defeat.

"My MP...!"

Mii was no more cost-efficient than Maple.

She'd been using Flare Impetus this whole time, right after using a number of big moves, and her Item Pouch was out of potions.

She could only use one more spell.

"......Immolate."

Mii gave up on running and turned back toward Maple, who was right behind her.

And then her body burst into flame.

"Er...trying to take me with you?!"

But even as Maple spoke, Mii's body turned into a towering column of fire that seemed to scorch the very sky, enveloping both her and Maple.

This was the only spell she had left that stood a chance.

But as she turned to ash, the last thing Mii heard was...

"Self-destruct skills don't work on me!"

...Maple's merciless cheer.

When the flames died down, Maple was the only one left standing.

"With all my skills, my VIT is almost at five digits! I knew that wouldn't work!"

She put her armaments away and called Syrup, who was

still carrying the twins, back down to earth and hopped aboard herself.

"If I'd known there would be so many traps, I'd have stayed in the air!"

"Let's grab the orb and head to the next location!"

"Sounds good. I really didn't want to use that skill, either. They made me do it!"

But when they reached the Flame Empire's pedestal, they found neither orbs nor players.

"Huh?"

"Wh-what does this mean?"

".........They took the orbs and ran?"

A stolen orb would only come back once the thief took it to their base and kept it there long enough to earn points. This process could take a while.

Mii's plan avoided that worst-case scenario, which meant Maple had wasted her time fighting here.

"Wh-what now? The whole point was to steal their orbs... argh..."

"Um. Well, there's one thing we can do..."

"What?" Maple listened avidly.

"There's a lot of guilds around here," Yui said. "If we take them out while looking for whoever has this guild's orbs..."

"...Ooh, yeah! That sounds good."

The wandering trio steamrolled every guild they found with a simple frontal assault.

Countless players were chewed up and spit out. The twins' attacks shattered sword and shield alike, as well as the players bearing them.

Six guilds were demolished in rapid succession, all because of their proximity to the Flame Empire base and Mii's gambit.

Flame Empire had evacuated quickly, and Maple's team never caught up.

"If we hide long enough, Maple will ensure the area around our base is safe," Mii said, after she respawned.

She was using Maple to eliminate the competition at the loss of the points they would have gained from properly defending their own orb, and the points they could have earned by stealing their neighbor's.

"That hurts...but there are benefits to it as well. And we know better than to mess with Maple again..."

Flame Empire headed to distant pastures, snatching as many orbs as they could while they waited for the Maple menace to vacate their home ground. They were soon engaged in a fierce battle with another powerful guild.

And the second night would bring some twists of its own.

CHAPTER 6

Defense Build and New Formations

As the sun set, all Maple Tree members were assembled at their base.

"Maple crushed the bulk of the Flame Empire's traps, and it'll take them a while to get back up to speed. That said, them running off with their orbs sure hurt."

"Sorry, Sally. We searched for a while, but no luck."

"Not a problem if Flame Empire are running wild to make up the points, but…we'll see."

The reason Maple had targeted them in the first place was to provoke Flame Empire into eliminating guilds that outranked Maple Tree.

If their guild was going to make the top ranks, they needed the big guilds to devastate everyone else.

Small guilds were being eliminated faster than they'd expected, and there were a lot of fights breaking out between midsize and larger guilds. They'd been using the midsize guilds to shake up the field, but the effectiveness of that stratagem was swiftly fading.

*　　*　　*

Maple Tree's goal was to land in the top ten.

The reward for doing so was the same regardless of whether you were first or tenth, so they weren't being *too* ambitious.

Currently, they were in sixth place.

The rest of the list was invariably all large guilds, so they stuck out like a sore thumb.

"I mean, we knew it would be like this, but the sheer number difference—we just can't keep up with them in a simple game of capture the orb."

"We're still doing better than expected. Honestly, I didn't think we'd be performing so well."

But even with Sally back in peak condition, it was a long way to the top.

"It's only day two, so catching up is still possible. It's just…we can't let the gap widen any more than it already is."

After discussing things a little more, they decided to leave Iz and Kanade on guard duty and have everyone else out conducting night raids.

One team was Sally, Mai, and Yui.

The other was Maple, Kasumi, and Chrome.

A team with Maple would basically never lose. Chrome and Kasumi could safely rack up points, while Sally could experiment and see how useful the twins were on sneak attacks. They'd trained together often, so the three of them could coordinate well, and Sally's skills were excellent for decoy work, keeping the enemy's attention on her.

"See you later!"

"Have fun! Kanade and I will be waiting right here."

Everyone had a copy of Sally's map, and the plan was for each team to pick a guild, attack it, and come straight back.

In the spectator zone, the topic of the hour was on just how *many* players had been eliminated. Night raids and surprise attacks had been chewing through the event's player base.

"Most guilds are gonna be out before we hit the halfway point."

"Totally possible. The small guilds are already running on fumes. Well, except Maple Tree, obviously."

They were the sole exception. Everybody checked the ranks again.

"Think they'll really stay in the top ten?"

"Flame Empire's struggling, too. Some of the top runners are definitely showing cracks here and there. The Order of the Holy Sword are stable, but I'm not so sure Maple Tree are."

"Yeah, they crumble once and they're done. It's an uphill battle for sure."

"But with Maple's defense, will they ever crumble?"

The spectator who mentioned it'd be a tough fight no matter what made a face.

"Maple's strong if she and her guildmates can force a fight. Make it so their opponents can't get away."

"Well, everyone's gotta defend their orbs, and if they lose 'em, they gotta at least try to get them back...so that's a strong maybe?"

"It is *Maple* we're talking about here."

Once someone said that, everyone started nodding.

It was a phrase that always ended conversations.

"Other than that, it's a question of whether the numbers difference will carry the day or not."

"They've come this far, so I hope they hang in there! If it's only big guilds, that'd be so dull."

"I get that, but...they've gotta be running low on supplies."

"Good point. That really would be the end of the line for them..."

Ultimately, everyone was expecting the top ten to be all big guilds. Lots of eliminated players were rooting for the guilds that took 'em out, which meant lots of cheers for Flame Empire and the Order. And some were definitely still watching Maple Tree's progress.

But despite the audience's predictions, back at the Maple Tree base, Iz was crafting a *ton* of potions.

Sally's team were hiding in the bushes, waiting for their chance to attack their target.

While they'd been waiting for Maple and the twins to wrap up the Flame Empire assault, Sally had sparred with Kasumi, trying to gauge how much her all-important evasive capabilities had deteriorated due to fatigue.

The results had suggested she was almost back in full swing, so she'd deemed herself ready to head back out.

"Hokay...go!"

Sally darted out of the brush, making a beeline for the orb.

"Enemy attack! Get some!"

"Okay...! I can see 'em!"

Sally dodged the incoming attacks, slicing players, moving closer to her target.

"Surround that thief! Cut off any escape routes!"

These people were organized. The defenders were quickly moving into position.

"Focus on me, and you'll miss the real threat…," she murmured.

That was when a shock wave hit a nearby player, shattering him instantly.

Someone else turned to gape, and Sally cut him down, forcing their attention back on her.

Everyone knew there was something lurking in the underbrush—still, they had no choice but to keep their eyes on Sally.

Naturally, they were slow to react when Mai and Yui popped out of the bushes.

Players facing away from them were hit in the back by the iron spheres the twins threw, dying without even knowing what had hit them.

Everyone who saw this happen understandably freaked the hell out.

These attacks were every bit as mind-boggling as Maple's own and effectively shut down organized enemy resistance.

"Oboro, Shadow Clone!"

Pile on another mind-boggling sight while they were still stunned and recovering became virtually impossible.

By the time the defenders tried to do something about the clones Sally had summoned, they were in range of the twins' hammers.

With a dull thud, their hammers sent multiple players flying into the air where they exploded into shards of light.

"H-how…?!"

""Double Stamp!""

Mai and Yui were making swift work of the crowd.

It went without saying that even if anyone managed to strike back, they were finished, but their minds were still reeling, and no one so much as tried. Anyone who *did* make a move would have to turn their back on Sally, and she wasn't about to let them do *that* unscathed.

Spotting players who were going after the twins was not a challenge for her at all.

Sally had kept the twins safe with an approach that couldn't be any more removed from Maple's.

She and the hammer girls all had their Vitality at default values, meaning a single hit would be the end of them.

But with the control of the flow of battle squarely in their hands, that would never come to pass.

"Now we just take their orb...and try a few more iron spheres next time."

""Got it!""

They headed to their next destination.

Kanade and Iz were alone at the guild base with plenty of time on their hands.

"All the guilds near us have already given up, huh? That's a bit boring."

"It's always possible guilds far from home won't know who we are... Oh, here we go."

Speak of the devil. A group of players filed down the entrance hall.

And the player in front glanced at their gear and quickly identified them as a crafter and back line support.

"We're good to go! They don't have any tanks or fighters!"

The attackers pressed forward, swords and shields at the ready.

"Shall we?"

"Let's."

Iz had a bomb in each hand while Kanade was flanked by bookshelves.

Maple Tree wanted to play aggressive, but they weren't settling by leaving these two on defense.

They knew full well the two of them could handle anything.

Iz flung her bombs toward the advancing enemy, who could only watch as the explosives multiplied in the air above them.

Blinded by explosions and flying bodies, the attackers ducked beneath their shields, trying to weather the rolling shock waves…

But the extra bombs were merely an illusion Kanade had created.

The actual number remained unchanged, and the extras did no damage.

So why waste MP on this? Well, because Akashic Records had spit out that skill, and Kanade had full use of it for the day.

No use being stingy with it. And he could always turn it into a grimoire later.

The other reason was simple—it bought them time.

After a short while, the explosions died down, and everyone could see again. They raised their weapons, ready to retaliate. However, Kanade already had a crackling white sphere floating in front of him.

"*Whew…*made it."

The sphere steadily grew smaller, falling in on itself. Sensing danger, the attackers tried to take cover. Then, a blinding light burst forward explosively.

This skill was called Calamity Cannon.

It had a long start-up time and a limited range, but it was strong beyond belief. That blinding light vaporized everything in front of him.

When it faded, the invading party was split in two—the spell had carved a path right down the center of their formation.

"Iz, I don't wanna blow too many grimoires, so..."

"Okay, here you go."

She pulled a bottle out of her pouch, filled with a black liquid, and handed it to Kanade.

This was another item New Frontier allowed her to create. It provided a massive boost to MP recovery for a short time.

Kanade chugged it, and as their opponents staggered back to their feet, several new magic circles appeared before their eyes.

It was a simple threat.

Leave...or die.

"Argh, to hell with this! Retreat!"

Shields up, they backed away down the hall, but more than a few of them were given a swift funeral as the pending spells went off.

Their hasty retreat was ultimately a success, mostly because Iz and Kanade hadn't given chase. If the twins had been there, by the time the attackers realized this guild wasn't so vulnerable after all, they would've all been dead. Same if Maple had been on guard duty.

"My supply of good grimoires is limited, so I'm glad they made up their minds so fast."

Kanade had been diligently converting the daily skills Akashic Records offered into grimoires, but those were generated randomly, and they weren't always what he was after. There were plenty of spells with no clear use.

Naturally, he had several spells as strong as Calamity Cannon, but like he mentioned, those were finite.

"There's always a chance a big guild like the Order will come after us, so I've gotta keep the best grimoires in reserve."

This time, the enemy had turned around quick—but next time, they might not be so lucky.

Still...as day two rolled on, many guilds were starting to worry about their mounting deaths, which resulted in many deciding to play it safe and retreat.

Meanwhile, Maple's party were soaring across the skies on turtleback. Kasumi, Chrome, and Maple had quite a large gap in terms of mobility, so if they were traveling together, this was the best way for them to keep pace as a group.

"Lately, everyone starts using piercing skills the moment they see me..."

"I certainly would."

"Same."

Maple's reputation preceded her, and it had become a well-known fact that you had to get past her defense if you wanted to do any damage.

This definitely made things harder for her (compared with the first event anyway). Even if they didn't manage to take her down, her whole goal had been to *not* get hurt.

"If I'm surrounded, Pierce Guard alone won't do it... Any ideas?"

Pierce Guard could null piercing damage, but it didn't last long.

"I'd say spray poison around you to make them back off, but everyone's been grabbing Poison Resist first chance they get..."

By this point in the conversation, they were nearing their target guild.

"Let's hop down!"

"...Sure."

"...Why not?"

Chrome and Kasumi each took one of Maple's hands and prepared to dive.

Maple's skill prevented them taking any damage from this, but it was still a stomach-churning drop.

"This doesn't faze you at all?" Kasumi asked.

"I wouldn't be able to do it in real life—but here, it never hurts!"

Hearing this, Chrome had one thought—

—he could *never* imitate the mindset that had earned Maple all her outlandish skills.

Anyone who wanted truly unique skills had to fundamentally think like nobody else.

And with that in mind...

The three of them plunged two dozen yards without a chute.

"Your orb is ours!"

With her Predators and party members guarding her, it was hard for piercing skills to hit Maple.

But since her angel form was protecting Chrome and Kasumi, their opponents had to take out Maple to hurt anyone.

"Huh," Chrome muttered. "Doesn't seem like there was anything to worry about."

Maple had been asking for advice on how to counter piercing damage, but she clearly already had it handled.

Frankly, Chrome couldn't even imagine someone giving Maple serious trouble.

Many a player came after Kasumi and Chrome, but they dodged, blocked, or parried, ending the battle with minimal pressure on Maple herself. It was a small guild, so there weren't many players to begin with, and they wiped out the defenders too fast for anyone to grab the orb and flee.

Once they were done, they hopped back on Syrup and headed to the next orb. Maple kept increasing altitude, making it so her turtle couldn't be identified from below.

Their maps made the various base locations clear, so they didn't need to rely on their eyesight. Before long, they were hovering over their target.

"Aw, there's no orb here," Maple said, peering over the edge.

Indeed, the pedestal was empty.

Nor were there any players. Either their orb had been stolen, or they'd been eliminated completely.

"Guess we could search the area?"

"I'll join you."

Chrome and Kasumi carefully investigated the surroundings but found no players or orbs.

"Nope, nothing. Guess we should head out."

"Yep, let's move on."

Three times they scanned camps from the skies above and didn't find a single orb.

Syrup's flight speed was hardly jetlike, so this had wasted a considerable amount of time.

The fruitless search and travel took a lot out of them as well.

As they flew farther, Maple heard the sound of an incoming message.

"Hmm... Oh, it's from Sally!"

She had informed everybody her group was headed back to base, and if Maple's crew wasn't having much luck, then they should come back, too.

Maple relayed Sally's suggestion, and they agreed to return home as well.

There were only a few hours left in the day, so it was about time anyway.

When they landed outside their base and tried to enter, they saw some strange players fleeing the passage, looking over their shoulders the whole way.

Just as they thought they'd escaped with their lives, they saw Maple waiting outside for them. Their faces crumpled as Chrome and Kasumi swiftly cut them down.

"We're under attack!"

"Yeah. Let's hurry!"

Kasumi took the lead, rushing toward their orb room. She burst in, katana raised, only to find five familiar occupants, Sally included.

Mai and Yui were busy retrieving iron spheres. They'd clearly just finished wiping out most of the intruders.

"You're all safe...," Kasumi observed, sheathing her blade.

Once Chrome and Maple caught up, the whole guild was back together.

Kanade and Iz were flopped out on the ground, worn out from defending while everyone else was out.

"So tired... Without Iz's items, we would've been sunk..."

"I used a *lot* of bombs... I'd better start making more."

Iz could use her workshop anywhere, so as long as she had time to craft, she'd never run out of items or ammunition.

"Hmm... Barely anyone even bothered coming close for ages. What changed?"

Like Maple pointed out, everyone had designated their base off-limits, so it was rather strange to suddenly have enemies trying their luck.

"Did you get any orbs, Maple?"

"Uh, no, not really. Lots of guilds with no orbs. You?"

"Similar levels of devastation. Only managed to find two."

They put the orbs they'd found on the pedestal, and then Sally explained the reasoning behind her earlier message.

"Dread said he'd be back, right? I'm sure the Order of the Holy Sword'll make another run at us eventually. I figured they'd wait for night, but the pace of this event is faster than I expected, so I figured our current approach wouldn't carry us much further."

She brought up the current rankings and scrolled down.

When all members of a guild reached the five-death limit, a mark appeared next to their name, showing they'd been eliminated. Once virtually exclusive to small guilds, the mark was now starting to spread through the midsize ones.

A number of guilds had been playing very aggressively from the get-go, and the guilds that had lost their orbs were all on the warpath, drastically increasing the overall fatality rate.

Few guilds could defend against a determined attack without sustaining casualties, and as a result, most guilds weren't likely to last past the end of day two.

The survivors were guilds with players to spare—and *exceptions*.

With fewer guilds remaining on the map, there were also fewer orbs up for grabs.

Maple Tree was getting attacked because guilds were roaming so far from their starting position that they didn't even know who they were up against.

Mai, Yui, and Maple were just too slow to roam the map in search of orbs at this stage.

No matter how strong they were, they couldn't steal orbs that weren't there.

"I figured it would take a *bit* longer to reach this point, but if everybody's this fired up... My plan depended on us earning a slew of points in the early stages, but we didn't get as many as I'd hoped."

Sally had figured the midsize guilds would last for quite a bit longer, but with them disappearing at an alarming rate, the overall orb count had decreased dramatically, and the remaining guilds were all huge. It was clear chaos would reign.

"This is much earlier than I'd expected, but I think it's time we moved to the next phase."

Everyone was on board with this, and they began going over their new roles.

Once she had a handle on hers, Maple turned to Sally.

"Now we just...?"

"Yep," Sally responded instantly, already way ahead of her. "Wait for the Order."

Maple gulped and began double-checking the skills and weapons she had available.

Ten minutes before the next day began, Maple Tree was deciding the roster for the night's watch when the last visitors of the day arrived.

They tabled the discussion and brandished their weapons.

These foes could not be taken lightly.

Only fifteen players total, but four of them were the leaders of the Order of the Holy Sword.

Pain, Dread, Frederica, and Drag.

There was no real need for them to target Maple Tree.

Taking out guilds that stood a chance of catching up to them was one thing, but the Order had a commanding lead over the smaller guild.

Pain had brought all his best players here for one simple reason—they all wanted to fight Maple Tree and win.

Every one of them wanted to face a worthy rival—a guild that had the potential to surpass them.

Which was why they'd made sure everyone was assembled before attacking.

However, to convince the rest of the guild to approve this ultimately meaningless assault, they'd been forced to choose the time of day when Maple would be at her weakest. It went against their wishes, but that's just how guild politics went sometimes.

That was why they were here at the tail end of the day.

"Yoo-hoo! We meet again!" Frederica grinned, waving at Sally.

Sally didn't seem sure what to make of that.

"You don't look too tense. You do realize we're about to throw down for real, right?" Drag asked, drawing his big ax. He was clearly raring to go.

Cautiously, the Maple Tree members readied themselves for combat.

Dread was quietly focusing his mind, and when he saw the twins glaring at him, clearly eager for some payback, he drew his dagger.

And at the head of the raiding party stood a man with gold-studded white armor and a matching shield, blond hair, blue eyes, and a powerful presence—the man known as Pain.

"Maple, I've been looking forward to facing you. And I believe I can win, so I'm here to take you down."

He drew a longsword that glittered in the dim light, raising it and his shield together. Even to Sally's keen eyes, his stance was flawless.

"Well, I don't like to lose!" Maple exclaimed as she popped a Doping Seed into her mouth. "Martyr's Devotion! Predators!"

Angel wings spread wide as her twin monsters reared up—and so battle was joined.

*　*　*

"Multi-Hasten!"

Frederica started the battle off by buffing her guildmates' speed.

Dread, Pain, and Drag stepped forward.

""Farshot!""

"Won't work twice."

Dread easily dodged the twins' rapidly expanding shock waves.

He was far too good at evasion for them to challenge him head-on.

And his earlier death had made him very aware of how unusual they were—important information he'd taken home with him.

This meant Mai and Yui had lost their greatest asset: the fact that nobody knew anything about them yet.

No one here was foolish enough to block their instakill attacks with a shield.

And since the twins were the front of the party, Drag started with them.

"Ground Wave!"

He slammed his ax into the ground so hard it sent a shock wave running through the earth, splitting it open and spraying bits of dirt like buckshot, battering Mai and Yui with the debris.

Thanks to Maple, they took no damage, but Drag's Knockback Bestowal trait was another matter.

It knocked Maple backward, leaving the twins outside the range of Martyr's Devotion.

This was no coincidence. Drag and Dread were already lunging toward the twins.

All of Maple Tree had fought hard that day. Maple and the twins, in particular, had shown a lot of their tricks in the battle against Flame Empire.

The Order's scouts had been watching that exchange very closely, without Maple noticing.

So they all knew:

The angel form's weakness.

About Maple's weapon deployment.

And that her great-shield skill—Devour—had a use limit.

All these bits of intel had fed into their plan to claim her head.

"Like I said! We *know* we can win!"

"Cover Move!"

"Not on my watch!"

"Magic Barrier!"

Kasumi squared up against Dread, Chrome stood in Drag's path, and Kanade threw up magical defenses all along the line of battle.

Even if Maple stumbled, Kasumi and Chrome were still top players.

They knew how to handle enemy attacks.

"Maple! Cancel it!" Sally yelled.

"O-okay! Will do!" Maple yelled, and the angel wings folded away.

If their opponents knew the skill's weakness, then it was safe to assume they were also ready to pepper her with piercing damage.

In fact, the next several spells Frederica cast were all that type.

All of them were aimed right at Maple, forcing her to turtle behind her shield and preventing her from moving.

While Drag and Dread kept four people occupied just by themselves, Pain surged forward, headed right toward Maple, sword and shield in hand.

"As if I'd let you."

"Coming through."

Sally swung her daggers, and Pain parried one with his shield and deflected the other with his sword.

She kept herself between him and Maple, fully focused, not missing a move.

"Dread!" Pain yelled.

But all three guild leaders responded.

"Godspeed!"

"Berserk!"

Dread's skill made him vanish while Drag's eliminated the post-skill delay.

And even as they busted out their big moves, Frederica's voice rang out.

"Multi-Transfer!"

This was the ace in her grimoire—a spell that took all buffs on her party members and shifted them to Pain.

Pain's speed rocketed so high he vanished from sight.

"You're not getting through…!" Sally shouted, guessing his location and swinging her dagger. But her attack was parried, doing no damage.

"Godspeed."

Then Pain got even *faster* and blew right past Sally.

She could guess where he was but couldn't actually catch him.

It came down to a difference in levels.

Pain's level was more than double Sally's, and his base stats were far higher.

In combat, she might be able to react and dodge better than he could, but that didn't have much effect if he wasn't trying to fight. Sally wheeled toward Maple, alarmed.

"Wh-where is he?!"

Maple had her great shield raised and was searching for him, her attention focused on her exposed side.

The shield was taller than she was, and she was certain it would protect her.

But that also made it a blind spot. She was shocked to hear a voice coming from the other side of her shield.

"Holy Condemnation!"

For a brief second, Pain held a glowing blade above his head— then he swung.

That stroke held the combined might of his allies, all aiming for Maple's head.

"Um…ah…"

She'd only felt this a handful of times, and for a moment, she couldn't think.

Pain's blade cut through her summoned Predators, cleaved her shield in two, and shattered her armor, gouging deep into Maple's body. She was flung toward the wall with only a single hit point left.

The sound of Maple slamming against the wall and the realization that she'd actually sustained fatal damage left all the Maple Tree members stunned and exposed.

The twins in particular were visibly shaken.

Chrome and Kasumi were hardly unaffected.

"Power Ax!"

"Gah…!"

Drag didn't let the chance slip by. His blade struck Chrome in the torso.

Frederica had been chain casting support spells from the rear, raising Drag's already high DPS even further. Nobody could take a hit from that head-on and live.

Like it had for Maple, Indomitable Guardian kicked in, allowing

Chrome to escape instant death with a single hit point, but he was still in serious trouble.

He wanted to go back up Maple, but Drag wasn't about to let that happen.

So Chrome changed tactics. His job now was to keep Drag from reaching Maple.

That was when Drag saw Chrome's HP bounding back. His eyes went wide.

"Damn, you're pretty tough yourself!" he shouted.

But with all these spells flying around, Chrome also had to guard the twins. That obviously wasn't tenable and wouldn't last for long.

Pain wasn't going to give Maple time to recover, either.

He'd hoped she didn't have Indomitable Guardian, but clearly she did.

Pain quickly gave chase. Drag's Berserk skill was active, canceling the delay after a skill use, so he was already moving to close the gap.

"Smog!"

Kanade's magic obscured Pain's vision. Anything that might stop him from reaching Maple was on the table.

Then Iz threw a bomb. The explosion was deafening.

"Holy Banishment."

A single swing of Pain's sword and the smoke vanished. His gaze turned toward them.

"No time...!"

"I can still...!"

Kanade tried to grab another grimoire, and Iz readied a new bomb, but Pain was far faster.

Without even breaking his stride, he cut down the back-liners and was only a few steps from Maple herself.

"Holy Breach."

He was surprised to see Maple's equipment restored but, intent on making it the final blow, quickly used an armor-piercing skill.

Pain was so focused that what happened next seemed to play out in slow motion.

Maple was slumped against the wall, her left side hidden behind her shield—but then the shield toppled forward.

And the hand behind it…was a cannon.

Belatedly, he realized that the smog and explosions had disguised her transformation.

"Not now…!"

Pain's skill was active. He *couldn't* dodge. All he could do was follow through with his swing.

"Counter!"

This skill was the new trick Maple had acquired in the third event.

When she took damage, she could stack the force of that attack onto her own.

Faster than Pain's swing, light burst from her cannon, searing his body.

His strongest blow had been reflected back at him.

"Gah…I'm not finished yet…!"

Pain, too, was left with a single hit point. Once again, he lunged at Maple.

*   *   *

"Holy Schism!"

"Atrocity!"

Where Maple had just been slumped against the wall, black mist appeared, taking shape.

And now *she* had the reach advantage. Pain's eyes went wide as her arms reached for him.

"What the......?!"

He sliced off her first arm and blocked the second grasping hand with his shield.

He survived the first two attacks.

But his foe wasn't *human*.

"My haste has spelled my defeat."

A hideous maw loomed—and bit him in two.

But Maple didn't stop there. She kept going, bearing down on Dread and Drag with terrifying speed.

"Seriously?! Is this real?!"

"Uh…how many forms does she have?"

And as they reeled with fear and confusion, the monster belched fire. They flinched, and a hideous arm grabbed Dread even as the maw closed around Drag.

"Is it weird that I feel relieved? Go on, finish me."

Dread closed his eyes, resigned to death by devouring.

Seeing the Order's three top players downed one after another, the attackers bringing up the rear knew they'd lost and wisely elected to beat a hasty retreat.

"I'm running, too! Multi-Hasten!"

But even as Frederica got the speed buff cast, Maple leaped over their heads, clinging to the wall behind them.

Her head loomed over the exit, drool dripping from her maw.

The only way out was through...*that.*

It didn't seem remotely possible, but before she could think of a new plan, Frederica heard the twins yell a skill name.

""Farshot!""

"! Multi-Barrier!"

Frederica threw out a spell...and immediately regretted it.

Defensive barriers were no use against Mai and Yui. In her haste, she'd opted for her go-to defense—

But their shock waves broke right through all her barriers and turned her to light.

Keeping Maple's Atrocity a secret had secured them the victory.

Without that skill, Pain's last swing would definitely have finished Maple off.

The front line had been wavering, and their entire line of battle would have crumbled in short order.

Sally would have pushed herself to the brink again, of course, but the Order of the Holy Sword undoubtedly had the upper hand.

Maple chewed her way through the rest of the attackers that remained, and while they waited for Iz and Kanade to revive, Sally picked up their orb.

"C'mon, Maple. Phase two."

"Oh! Right!"

The witching hour was approaching.

Her monster form melted into the darkness.

And seven more monsters rode upon her back, bent upon guild destruction.

CHAPTER 7

Defense Build and the Dark of Night

In a darkened forest, a large guild was defending their base by torchlight.

"Guilds are dropping like flies..."

"Yeah, not long till the big guilds will be forced to wage war against one another. No telling when someone'll show."

They heard a rustle from the brush.

"...Come on."

"Yeah, better check it out."

They drew their swords and cautiously approached the source of the sound.

And when their lights reached the brush, they found the head of a monster, its mouth open wide.

""......Huh?""

Before they could react, it swallowed them whole.

This nightmare had only just begun. The monster's rampage carried it into the heart of their base.

By the time the defenders realized something was wrong, they were ripped apart, bitten in half, or burned to a crisp.

Given the size of their guild, the initial casualties were hardly significant, but the psychological impact was extreme, and the survivors were unable to mount any organized resistance.

They were prepared for enemy armies to invade, but none of them were ready for a single nightmarish monster running amok.

"This event has boss monsters?!"

"Nobody ever tells me nothin'!"

"It's after me! What do I do?!"

Chaos was spreading like a wildfire. Orders were given, and nobody listened.

Seven players jumped down from the creature's back, picking off defenders in the turmoil punctuated by screams of terror.

The sight of this hideous monster eating their companions was so engrossing that few defenders even noticed the other visitors.

By the time they realized the monster was not alone, half the guild had already been slain.

"Okay, next!" Sally yelled.

The monster stopped gorging itself, let the seven climb aboard, and left the guild behind. Any players who stood in her way were torn limb from limb.

"Cool, got the orb! This is going well."

"Where to now?"

"Hmm, let's go...left."

Maple was in full Atrocity mode while Sally rode on her back.

Their goal was to crush as many big guilds as they could before news about Maple's last and greatest form spread—and before anyone could plan countermeasures.

She was a brand-new natural disaster, and nobody was prepared.

They'd swiped the orb, killed half the guild, and left before any-one even worked out what was happening.

Maple had sacrificed humanity in exchange for mobility, and she spent the night laying waste to absolutely anything she could get her grotesque appendages on.

In monster form, she had two big advantages: Firstly, nobody knew this was Maple, and secondly, she didn't let anyone live long enough to consider using piercing skills.

And she had Sally directing her, calling for a timely retreat before anyone had time to begin thinking about what attacks might be effective against the beast.

This plan was a multipronged affair that aimed to steal orbs, whittle down their enemies, and sow untold devastation wherever they went.

One guild based in an open field had decided to weather the night by extinguishing their torches, hoping to keep a low profile. Many of the largest guilds had large, exposed bases, and the fields had proven the least defensible terrain.

"Not much moonlight tonight, either... Sure is dark."

"I thought as much during the second event, too. It's hard to do anything after sunset."

Time passed in silence.

The only sounds filling the night air were insects chirping, the wind, and other guild members talking softly.

So it was hard to miss the sound of something running toward them.

"Lights! Light it up!"

Light spells shot toward the sound—revealing a gargantuan monster, the likes of which no one had seen yet in this event.

As the lights hit it, the beast breathed fire, causing a shudder to run through the entire guild.

Few things before or after shook them quite as much as this.

Nobody knew what to do.

"This is ours!" the monster yelled, grabbing their orb.

"You can have these instead."

The seven figures on her back started throwing various objects at them.

And as the explosions rang out in a continuous staccato, iron spheres, shock waves, and spells joined them.

Before large-scale combat even began, ten players had been eaten, twenty were felled by raining fire, and quite a few more were simply trampled to death on the monster's way out.

"Before the night is done, we've gotta take out as many as we can before word spreads."

"You betcha!"

This plan could net them a bunch of points, but more importantly, it would hasten the complete destruction of the larger guilds.

The event was progressing at breakneck speed to begin with, and this would only accelerate it—all to ensure they'd stay in the top ten when the final day came.

Even if that proved impossible, based on the success of this strategy so far, Sally was certain they could send the event into hyperdrive.

"Maple, hang in there a bit longer!"

"Gotcha! I'm still good to go!"

Maple raced toward their next target, never slowing down.

After watching the battle between Maple Tree and the Order of the Holy Sword, everyone in the spectator zone spoke of nothing else.

"Maple actually won!"

"But it could have gone either way. I was sure Pain had won when he blew her away."

"The Order basically had it in the bag. It really was that final shocker that clinched it."

"No telling what would happen if they clashed again! Still… Maple's gone insanely left field. She *left* the damn field!"

"Yeah… You can't exactly call her an angel anymore…"

They were, of course, talking about Atrocity. The silence after her transformation had been palpable. Literally no one could believe their eyes.

"Where'd she even find that skill?"

"…Who knows. I can imagine why Pain was shocked!"

"How does that thing move?! With all those limbs…"

"I don't think I could even walk in that form."

"Either way, this means Maple Tree have a real shot at ranking. I mean, if even Pain can't do it, who can?"

"You've gotta come prepared with more than just Poison Resist. Like, seriously, most bosses are easier."

"You can say that again. But I'm glad I saw it with my own eyes! Proof that Maple *can* be damaged! The concept of HP applies even to her!"

"I hope those two fight again somewhere. Just…not near me."

Everyone present nodded in hearty agreement.

"Still, the monster thing is *nuts*."

Everyone nodded again, with emphasis.

The massacre continued unabated all night long, ending at six the next morning.

Maple Tree piled the orbs they'd stolen on their pedestal, put their own orb back in place, and declared the operation was complete.

"Whew…I'm bushed! I haven't run that far…ever…"

Maple was *still* in monster form.

Thanks to Sally's sharp eye for potential threats, she'd taken little to no damage…but fatigue was another matter.

"Is it all right if I get some shut-eye? If anything happens, you can just come and wake me up."

"Yeah, it's fine. You get some rest."

Maple headed down the hall—without dropping Atrocity.

Seemed a shame to let it dissipate unless she had to.

Atrocity could only be used once a day.

"If any big guilds roll in, then the plan is to just back off so we don't lose anyone?"

"Yep, that's right. We'll grab our orb and take it straight to Maple."

Since Maple Tree was classified as a small guild, the guilds they'd robbed were due for a significant point loss, and odds were high some would be willing to risk an attack to avoid that.

Maple Tree currently possessed ten orbs.

Seven belonged to big guilds.

And since all of them would have to come here to get their orbs back, there was a solid chance they'd clash before they even reached Maple Tree.

If they *didn't* come after the orb, it was probably because they were busy attacking some other guild.

Whatever happened to these orbs in the end, a *lot* of players would die.

And since Maple Tree were trying to speed up the event's progression, this carnage was more valuable than any points they might get from the orbs themselves.

It didn't really matter if they managed to defend them or not.

"I think we've got a solid shot at the top ten. We got off to a good start."

"That means we've gotta focus on staying alive. Let's see if anyone comes."

One eye on the entrance, they all did their best to ease the pent-up exhaustion.

Just after seven, some seventy-odd players came in, huddled behind a row of great shielders.

When they emerged from the narrow passage into the large room, they swiftly spread out, weapons raised. The orb pedestal was a good fifteen yards away, and they were playing it safe.

"...Think they're the winners of a fight?"

"Not sure. I think it's likely they lost some people on the way over, but..."

It was a *lot* of people, but...not for a large guild.

Maple Tree's formation had Sally, Chrome, and Kasumi at the fore, avoiding the area in front of the twins.

Iz was standing between Mai and Yui while Kanade brought up the rear.

The berth they gave the twins was to give them room to freely throw iron spheres.

""Hyah!""

The attackers had seen quite a lot of combat, and their shields simply couldn't withstand those thrown missiles.

"More," Iz said, pulling additional spheres out of her inventory as fast as the twins could throw them. They wouldn't run out of ammo any time soon.

But powerful tanks and sheer numbers meant the attackers were still making progress.

Mai and Yui could one-shot anyone, but they could only throw one sphere at a time, so there were plenty of people not getting hit at all.

And of course, front-line fighters were prime magic targets. A wave of spells shot toward them—

"Cover Move!"

Chrome vaulted in front of them, tanking the attack spells with shield and body.

He took a lot of damage, but his shield and skills quickly restored it.

As long as Chrome didn't die, simply standing still would start healing him, which made him incredibly hard to kill.

He spent a lot of time in Maple's shadow, but he was a nightmare to handle in his own right.

"Frozen Land."

Kanade activated a pale blue grimoire, encasing the advancing forces in ice that reached up to their ankles.

They were only stuck for five seconds...

But that was an eternity when the twins were nearby.

Shields snapped one after another while armor creaked and cracked—all bad things that would make future combat brutal given the rules of this event.

Many players were already falling back. Their losses kept mounting.

"Oboro, Shadow Clone."

Sally's clones were dashing about, attacking everyone within sight.

She wasn't really built for defense or crowd control, so she mostly played support or used her skills to sow chaos and shake enemy morale whenever the opportunity presented itself.

Kasumi spent her time warping up to enemy tanks, cutting them down, and then using Leap to withdraw before anyone could retaliate. Classic hit-and-run.

Each of them had their own strengths, and as long as they could use them to their fullest, mobs of average players just wouldn't cut it.

You had to meet a certain strength threshold to compete.

And with less than an hour of sleep, the sound of iron spheres thumping roused their leader.

There was a shuffling from down the hall, and a monster crawled out, rubbing its eyes. The would-be invaders shuddered. They knew it had attacked their guild but hadn't expected it to emerge from a back room like this.

"Would you all be quiet?! Do I have to beat you up again? Argh!"

This was a monster that was only created when someone who'd already crossed a certain threshold takes a strange turn off the well-trodden path. And with her guild backing her up—well, no one who hadn't even crossed that threshold yet stood a snowball's chance in hell against her.

An hour after that first raid...

Another two hundred players came filing in, and Maple Tree

decided to hand over all orbs in their possession except their own before dashing back inside. Their goal was to play it safe and keep all their members alive.

"If we've gotta lose them, it oughtta be a guild like that who should take 'em."

"Yeah...and from here on..."

The back room was a designated space for resting, but with Maple's Atrocity active, there wasn't much space left. They all listened close, seeing if the massive guild outside was planning on still coming after them.

If they did, they'd just have to wake up Maple. But these visitors seemed to know the rule about sleeping Maples and apparently decided not to chance it.

Stealing Maple Tree's orb was the same as letting Maple Tree know exactly where you were at all times.

A single orb was definitely not worth that risk. There was no need to deliberately provoke legitimate threats.

Five minutes after the enemy cleared out, Chrome was at the head of the party, putting their orb back on the pedestal.

"All right... Now we just have to hope the big guilds all take one another down," Sally muttered.

Kasumi sidled up to her, showing the current rankings.

"Judging from this, the midsize guilds are getting eliminated quick. We've definitely upped the pace."

Based on the numbers, by day four, almost no one besides the big guilds would be left in the running.

"We've let the orbs go for now. Let's give Maple some more time to rest."

"Agreed," Kasumi said.

They had a plan for after the orbs were gone. Sally was already headed out.

"I'll follow that guild. If it looks like they might get in another big scrap, then…"

She looked at Kanade.

"Yes, we can use your skills and mine…," he said.

"Also, bring Maple."

"Got it."

"Right, then! I'm outta here."

And Sally departed from the base.

They'd wake Maple in three hours, or if they got word from Sally, whichever came first.

"Doesn't seem like we'll be attacked by anyone else, so let's take this time to relax."

""Okay.""

Mai and Yui still had an important duty to fulfill.

It was vital they rest in preparation.

Sally caught up with the two-hundred-strong army relatively easily.

Moving en masse was a slow process. There were a limited number of routes they could take that wouldn't nullify their numbers advantage.

She'd predicted the most likely route based on that logic, and her guess had paid off in spades.

"Looks like they haven't run into any other guilds…yet."

Sally kept watch from a distance. She made sure they never spotted her, but she took care to not lose them, either.

Holding orbs meant the orbs' owners knew exactly where you were. And most of those owners were large guilds themselves.

Sally was pretty sure one of them would show eventually—and as she watched, two fireballs appeared.

"Oh? Coincidence…? Well, we definitely didn't take *their* orbs."

Flames scorched the earth and skies alike, turning unlucky players to ash.

The massive guild flung spells back, but one player dodged them all, taking advantage of her fire-powered Agility.

"Flame Empire…makes sense. Not a whole lot of guilds left, so any guilds trying to stay in the top ten will have to fight them eventually. I feel bad for Maple, but…"

Sally sent Chrome a message, telling her teammates to bring their orb and assemble at her location.

After easily dismantling a large guild all by herself, Mii took their orbs and headed toward her base.

Flame Empire was currently in fifth place.

Maple's assault had hurt them, or they'd have been a bit higher in the rankings. She'd destroyed a lot of Marx's traps and left their defense in tatters.

And as a result, a lot of their players had died or been eliminated completely.

"If we can just keep these orbs safe…"

Certain there was no immediate threat, Mii took an MP potion from her supply squad.

In time, they reached the Flame Empire base and set the orbs in place. She breathed a sigh of relief.

"Finding these was a stroke of luck…"

"But there's no telling who they belong to. And their owners are definitely coming after us," Misery said.

And whoever those foes might turn out to be, they'd get there before the orbs could get scored.

"Yes—call Shin over."

"Good idea."

They summoned everyone back to base and began preparing as best they could.

When Shin returned, Flame Empire's scout units were already reporting enemy movement.

They were headed this way and every last one of them were large guilds. Flame Empire's orb pedestal was surrounded by open fields. There was nowhere to hide.

And their foes knew exactly how powerful Flame Empire could be. None of them could win on their own, so they were teaming up, hoping to take out a major foe and then grab the prize for themselves afterward. This meant a makeshift alliance of several large guilds now had Flame Empire surrounded.

"They're coming! Brace yourselves!"

"Yeah... Here's hoping...!"

"Don't worry; Mii'll take care of it."

"I'll keep everyone healthy."

But even as the guild leaders prepared themselves, Mii got a new message.

Monster inbound. Likely Maple. Threat level high.

Mii read this, and the color drained from her face.

"You're kidding... Hasn't she done enough? This is ridiculous!"

A rare glimpse of her real persona. Her friends all looked concerned.

She relayed the message to them.

"I feel sick."

"Look...Kasumi might have taken me down, but... She won, but..."

"Ah. Right...yeah...," Marx muttered...and then he collapsed.

He already knew his traps didn't work on Maple.

"I feel sick," Misery said, again.

But the allied hordes were closing in.

◆□◆□◆□◆□◆

One guild after another appeared on their perimeter. Over a thousand players had gathered.

"......We're wiping either way. Might as well take as many as we can with us!" Mii roared.

She activated Flame Empress, steeling her nerves for the impending battle.

"You can do this. You *have* to do this," Marx muttered to himself, forcibly climbing to his feet. He slapped his own cheeks a few times to clear his mind and rouse his spirits.

"Right...here goes. Flare Impetus!"

With a fiery blast, the battle began. Spells rocketed toward Flame Empire from all directions.

But they were up against several large guilds—it wouldn't be *only* spells.

"Saint's Prayer!"

Misery's spell made light pour from the heavens.

It cost all her MP and left her unable to recover MP for the next three minutes—but in exchange, it provided high-speed auto-healing over a massive area for a set period of time.

Any of her guild members who took damage recovered rapidly; it would take a lot of sustained damage to kill anyone.

Big moves like this had major cooldowns, so even once she managed to restore her MP, she couldn't use it again.

But this was definitely the time to bust it out.

"The rest is yours," Misery said.

She would be out of commission for a while and relying on her team.

"We've got this," Shin said. Mii had gone one way, so he and Marx went the other. Dividing their forces weakened them, but the situation left them with no choice.

"Detonate!"

The spells hurtling toward her were deflected by the force of the blast as Mii rocketed toward her enemies at speeds no other mage could manage.

Fireballs slammed into faces, and flames shot out of the ground, annihilating everyone around her.

But this came at a steep MP cost. To take all these foes out using her current methods would require more than the potions she had on hand.

"Nevertheless...!"

The more she *could* take down, the better their final standing would be.

Escape had never been an option. All she could do was push herself to the limit.

But then the thing she'd feared most arrived.

A giant monster was running across the field behind the enemy forces.

If she hadn't been in combat, Mii would've clasped a hand to her brow and stared up at the heavens.

"We're so...doomed..."

Or so Mii thought. Her supposed enemy had other plans, however.

When the monster reached the alliance's rear lines, it tore into them, ripping the players apart.

The monster blew in like a merciless storm, leaving chaos and calamity in its wake.

"We're still in this…?!"

Mii focused once more, fighting tooth and nail.

Maple Tree's goal was the destruction of the guilds swarming Flame Empire.

And to that end, they were doing their best to help Flame Empire keep their stronger players alive.

In other words, they were here to save Mii, Marx, Misery, and Shin.

Maple Tree needed all four of them to wreak untold havoc.

And Mii had enough sense not to try and stop Maple's rampage.

Maple herself went nowhere near Mii.

Functionally, they were now fighting on the same side.

"Keep it going!"

"Okay!"

Everyone on her back hurled explosives, expanding the carnage. Maple herself just kept trampling the armies, tearing players apart.

"Maple! Trouble that way!"

"I see it!"

Her monster form was sinister enough in the dark, but in broad daylight, it was downright terrifying.

Enough that Maple was drawing the attention of all the large guilds.

Without any of them discussing it, they all turned their blades toward her, acting purely on instinct.

She was a threat they had to take out immediately, even if it meant ignoring Flame Empire.

"Oh…that's a *lot* of enemies!"

"Yep. Uh, Maple? Protection!" Sally squeaked.

Maple activated Martyr's Devotion, and everyone around was bathed in its light. Even as it kicked in—

"Atrocity's down! Hngg… Hey, gimme a second!"

Seeing her spill out of the monster, the nearby players saw their chance and lunged, only to be met by Maple's shield—and Devour. This was a good reminder that Maple was a major threat even without Atrocity active. She quickly swallowed several foes and then made sure everyone in her party was safe and sound.

"Everyone's good! But…"

A few seconds earlier, Sally had spotted Pain behind a tree, blade drawn. He had a robe over his head, but there was no mistaking that distinctive glowing white longsword.

He, too, had heard that all-out war had broken out and was here to eliminate competition. He might not have been after them specifically, but he'd definitely shot a glare their way.

And with all eyes already focused on Maple and tons of players clustered around them, they were a prime target.

"Maple! Incoming! You'd better…"

"Yup! Atrocity!"

The previous day's transformation had run out, but she hadn't used *today's*.

The horror was reborn. And if that wasn't bad enough…

""Phantom World!""

Kanade and Sally yelled as one.

This spell created three autonomous clones of any target that would last for three minutes—with identical stats.

And of course, their target was Maple.

*　　*　　*

There were now *seven* Maple monsters.

Pain hadn't been the only one waiting in the wings. Drag, Frederica, and Dread were all present as well.

They'd all seen Maple revert to her original form and taken a step forward.

"She's worse every time I see her! Damn! Earth Splitter!"

Resignation in his voice, Drag split the ground.

Getting close to any of these Maples was far too dangerous, so he'd opted to slow them down instead.

The holy sword's light gleamed, the ground cracked open, flames erupted, and monsters rampaged.

Vines swarmed across the earth, spells arced through the sky, swords danced in the air, and illusions sowed chaos everywhere.

And as devastation took its toll, the flooding light of vanishing players gave the battlefield an eerie beauty.

"Crap! Death in every direction!"

"This is a disaster! Please, somebody make it stop!"

"Don't just stand there! There's two of them inbound!"

Some called out encouragement, while others abandoned themselves to their fate. But Maple's clones trampled all alike.

Mere mortals could not survive the arrival of hell on earth.

One after another went down. Three minutes later, when Maple's clones finally vanished—over half the alliance armies were gone.

But by this point, everyone had realized they could use piercing skills on her Atrocity form and had pinged her with minor damage enough times that she was forced back to her regular body.

The monster reared back, and Maple herself plopped out in front of the horde.

All of them readied their best skills. None of them planned to let her hit the ground.

"Full Deploy!"

But even as she fell, dozens of gun barrels sprouted out of her, aimed at the ground.

With a series of clangs, weapon after weapon appeared.

"Saturating Chaos! Hydra!"

They'd all seen enough monster maws to last them a lifetime, but Maple aimed another right at the players beneath her, instantly wiping them out.

And Hydra came right behind, coating the ground in poison—Maple's kind of terrain.

Anyone without prodigious Poison Resist melted.

Maple had lost her monster body, but she'd *always* been a monster. She merely looked human sometimes.

And that might be an understatement.

Her appearance might have improved, but she had access to far more varied attacks and was much harder to hit.

She was a devil with the face of an angel and far more of a nightmare to deal with.

That was the conclusion nearly all her foes arrived at.

When she landed, still bristling with weaponry, she began spinning in place, mowing down the crowds.

At the center of a lake of virulent poison, only players with

Poison Nullification could get close. Some players were casting ranged piercing spells, but her shield neutralized them.

The allied army quickly abandoned hope. The horde surrounding her melted away as everyone ran for it.

Maple wasn't about to let them escape that easily. There was a boom as she began rocketing around the battlefield.

The Order of the Holy Sword may have botched their surprise attack, but Earth Splitter tripped up everyone around them and allowed them to avoid retaliation.

Currently, they were after Flame Empire's orbs, and since all their competition were nice enough to gather in one place, they were carving a path through them.

Pain and Dread could each wreak havoc on their own, so they were fighting independently. Drag and Frederica were moving in tandem.

They were keeping their distance from Maple Tree, mostly because letting them continue their rampage was rather convenient for hurting their enemies, but also because Maple Tree members were *dangerous.*

"It'd be ideal if we could retreat before they target us…," Pain murmured, even as he cut down another player.

Like Maple, fighting players below a certain threshold was more routine work than anything else.

His mind was elsewhere, simulating a fight with Maple and picturing potential outcomes.

He concluded that no matter what he did, if both of them were operating at their peak, then he'd never take her down.

"I'll have to rework my build."

Pain fully intended to fight her again—when he was sure he could win.

"I'll have to find some new skills."

He glanced at her rampage out the corner of his eye, cut another player down, and decided the tide was turning. It was time for the Order to leave.

The three guilds every team feared had all gathered in one location.

The casualties were incredible.

And all three guilds had largely avoided fighting one another, which made it that much worse for everyone else.

When the tattered remnants of the allied army retreated, all that remained were the Flame Empire's four leaders and the members of Maple Tree.

Chrome had been keeping the twins and back-liners safe with Cover Move and Cover, leaving him running on fumes. Kasumi had been healing herself, and Sally never had a problem.

And obviously, Maple was fine.

"If it weren't for these skills, I would've been done for," Chrome said, amazed to find himself alive.

There were so many times he found his HP on the precipice, but Soul Eater, Soul Syphon, and Battle Healing had kept it bouncing back up at a genuinely alarming rate.

Meanwhile, Flame Empire's ranks were in tatters. They'd all used up every last trick they had. Worse, the bulk of their roster had been eliminated entirely.

They stood no chance against Maple Tree now.

Mii knew this perfectly well. Their orb sat between Maple and her team, but she did not even try to collect it. Flames shimmered around her...

And then there was a massive explosion.

She'd blown through the rest of her MP, copying Maple's

self-destruct flight to haul Misery, Shin, and Marx out of Dodge at blistering speeds.

The biggest different from Maple's approach was that Misery was healing her. They cut it close, but it worked as intended.

All Flame Empire guild members had been on board with it.

To stay in the top ranks, they'd trusted the guild's future to their four brightest flames.

And that was how Maple Tree got all their orbs back.

CHAPTER 8

Defense Build and Safe Territory

Since they were unable to use Atrocity again, Maple Tree wound up heading back to their base aboard Syrup.

They put all their orbs on the pedestal, and then everyone went to sleep.

About an hour later…

Normally, someone would have shown up by this point. But the event was going so fast, and everyone was worried about their death counts and possible elimination, so nobody wanted to voluntarily venture into the killing fields.

Despite the pile of orbs waiting here, Maple Tree's base was still, the quietest any part of the game had been since the event began.

"Sally? Whatcha lookin' at?"

Maple saw Sally with her screen open and came over.

"Mm? Oh, uh…things got *really* nuts."

"What do you mean?"

Maple leaned in, peeking at Sally's screen. It displayed the current rankings.

The biggest change was how the large guilds were starting to get eliminated.

"Oh, there goes another! Either the Order or Flame Empire has gotta be takin' 'em out. I think."

"Yeah?"

"My money's on Flame Empire. They were almost at death's door earlier. Probably won't last the remaining two days at this rate. So…their plan is to murder any threats in their immediate vicinity and leave the rest to fate."

She had no way of checking with them directly, but anyone Flame Empire eliminated wouldn't be able to earn any more points, which would theoretically keep the Empire in the top ten by default.

But they were definitely struggling to hang on, and attacking enemy guilds—especially large ones—would be a challenge, even if that was the sole way of keeping their current rank.

They couldn't keep this up for long.

"But the rate they're exterminating the competition is insane. They're going even faster than you did."

"I can't beat anyone who doesn't get close, so… Then again, if they don't get close, I don't get hit, either!"

Many players knocked aside by Maple in Atrocity mode didn't actually die from it. Most who did had been knocked in the wrong direction and were trampled a second time.

But getting launched through the air by a monster did tend to make people panic.

And while the sight of other players getting tossed around did sow terror and chaos, actually killing everyone in that crowd would take ages, even if she took full advantage of her size in monster form.

Maple also had a strong flair for "death by surprise" and had been enjoying this shock value; a month from now, it would not be so easy.

Meanwhile, Mii's fighting style was rather straightforward— she simply hit everyone as hard as she could.

Her DPS way far higher than Maple's.

And having learned the self-destruct flight trick from Maple, if she pushed herself, she could quickly wipe out a whole slew of major guilds.

Maple Tree was all in favor of this strategy.

"Nobody's coming to get these back...and once they score, we're pretty much guaranteed to be in the top ten."

"So we won't need to head back out?"

"Pretty much."

Maple grinned and sat herself down.

"This is *definitely* the most work I've ever done," she said. "I'm so tired!"

"Keep Crystal Wall and your armaments on hand, just in case."

"Mm, got it!"

Confident that Maple knew what to do, Sally sat down herself, and the two of them watched the other guilds die together.

Outside the game, the admins were staring at the list of remaining guilds.

"It's all over, huh?"

"Yup..."

There were now only six guilds still in play.

And all those guilds were ranked.

This meant the top ten guilds were set in stone.

An event planned to last five days had functionally ended on the morning of the fourth. The total guild number showed no signs of dropping further.

"Is our entire player base this bloodthirsty?!"

"Let's start editing a video of the highlights. Nothing else major's gonna happen after this point."

He started handing out orders, and the admins around started sifting through the massive volumes of recordings, picking out the key scenes.

"They're like...half Maple...," he muttered.

"You want us to find good footage she *isn't* in?" another admin asked incredulously. "We're already being super picky!"

The lead admin rubbed his temples, leaning back against his chair.

"Maple Tree stirring up the pot is *why* this event went so off the rails..."

"Flame Empire's ranked *tenth*—and already eliminated. We had them pegged as a top contender! You really can't predict these things."

They'd taken out a lot of rivals but pushed themselves too hard in the process and ultimately succumbed to their wounds.

Still, they'd managed to eke out a tenth-place finish.

"If only Maple was even remotely predictable..."

This was a thought shared by most players on the server.

It was much easier to handle someone if you knew what to prepare for.

"No use wishing for the impossible. More importantly, if we're doing another event like this, we'll have to reconsider the time span...and completely rethink how we handle the various guild sizes."

"Yeah, I didn't expect all-out war to break out on day two."

As he pondered the next step, another admin jumped up, speaking loud enough for everyone to hear.

"Place your bets! What is Maple doing *now*? Get it right, and I'll pick up your tab tonight!"

Everyone jumped on that offer.

There were no downsides.

"Recent footage should give us a clue... I've only got clips around their orb, though."

He pulled up a video of the Maple Tree base, from the fourth day.

"So she might *not* be in their base?"

"Totally possible! That'll make her hard to locate...but why would she leave?"

"Prediction time! Hand's up if you've got an idea!"

Several hands shot up.

The ringleader pointed at each in turn.

"Board games with all guild members!"

"Practicing Machine God flight."

"The twins are using her as a pinball!"

"Trying to get a skill by chewing on weapons Iz spat out!"

"These all sound way too normal."

"Fair..."

Everyone was silent for a minute, trying their best to think like Maple.

And of course, their predictions grew steadily wackier.

"She's made her turtle giant and climbed into its mouth!"

"Sally and her are fighting for...some reason."

"Biting the turtle!"

Everyone had a turn.

When they ran out of ideas and the room fell silent, the ringleader called it.

"Okay…pulling up the live feed."

"Hoo boy."

A moment later, the big screen showed the Maple Tree base…

Maple was covered in a ball of wool, with dozens of weapons poking out of it, and the twins were carrying her around the base.

Moments later, the admins quietly closed the video.

"…Add that to the highlights?"

"Why not."

The clip was calmly added to the end of the reel, and the staff took a moment to process a scene that no one could possibly understand.

Defense Build and Bonds

The admins were right—the event was already over.

Not a single fight happened after day four—peace reigned.

With no major changes in the rankings, day five came to an uneventful close. The remaining players in the event were swiftly transported back to the main game.

And a few moments later, each player saw a screen pop up in front of them, displaying the final results.

"Third again!"

"Oh, right, Maple. You were third in the first event, too."

Since all the top ten got the same reward, they hadn't made any special effort to finish at the top, but the points they'd earned from all the large guilds' orbs had pushed them several ranks up.

Their screens were now showing the reward.

Every guild member received five silver medals as well as a wooden token. And as the guild master, Maple received an item for display in their guild home—one that raised the stats of all members by 5 percent.

Maple put all these in her inventory, then took the token out again, looking it over.

"Access Permit: V... Hmm..."

Her name appeared in fine print below those words.

Clearly, these couldn't be passed around.

"These'll probably be used on the next stratum. Should be quite a while before we get a chance to use 'em, though," Sally said, putting her token away. "That aside...Maple, good work out there."

"You too, Sally!"

All Maple Tree members took a moment to congratulate one another, then they headed back to their guild home.

Maple suggested they have a party to celebrate their victory. Everyone was on board with that idea, so they picked a date and a venue—the Maple Tree home.

Iz had maxed her Cooking skill out, so the food was insane.

But when the promised hour arrived, everyone was there— except Maple.

"She ran out to buy something and never came back. Maybe I shoulda gone with her..."

"Yeah...if you leave her on her own, she'll just wander off."

Right as Sally stood up to go look for her, the door opened. Maple was back.

She had brought some surprising guests.

"I'm hooome!"

"Oh, there you are, Maple. What's all this?"

Sally peered over Maple's shoulder at none other than the leaders of the Order and Flame Empire.

Maple answered her question with great cheer.

"I bumped into them outside, and after we chatted for a bit, I somehow ended up friending them all and invited them over! This is exactly like how, you know, all the strong characters in stories always know one another! Apparently, I'm strong now!"

"Uh, right."

Maple had opened up her friends list. Just like she said, it had all members of Maple Tree, the four leaders of the Order of the Holy Sword, and the four leaders of Flame Empire listed.

Sally knew full well what other players thought about Maple and definitely saw this "friendship" in a different light.

It was a list that would make any last boss run screaming.

Iz handled the extra company in style, pumping out even more dishes.

Maple Tree only had eight members, so they had room for many more.

While everyone was enjoying the feast, they got a message from the admins.

It had a video attached.

"Let's put it up on the guild screen! We all got the same video."

Maple hopped up and fiddled with the big screen until she got the video playing.

It was a highlight reel of the event.

And almost all the footage was of people present.

First Pain, then Mii—then it cut to Sally.

"Oh! This was the night…when I screwed up…," Frederica wailed.

"If I hadn't been so tired, I'd have taken you out myself," Sally said.

Frederica looked hurt. "I'm not *that* easy!"

"Wanna go again, then?"

"Anytime! This time I'll hit you! I won't miss!"

And then it showed Maple.

"Still in human form."

"We know she's actually seven monsters."

Dread and Drag both shared blank stares as they rattled off those comments.

Chrome was the only one among the boys who hadn't died, so this was a hard video for them to watch. Kanade had somehow placed himself on the girl's side of the room, where he fit right in.

"Just thinking about it hurts," Marx muttered. It might be a while before he recovered.

Near the end, it was showing Chrome using his abnormal healing rate and Cover Move to warp around while guarding Mai, Yui, Iz, and Kanade. The glares he was getting screamed *I thought you were the* normal *one*.

"We'll win next time," Pain declared. "I'm not one to let a loss stand. And we know your skills intimately now."

"Man," Chrome said. "You take your eyes off her a second and she comes back as a furball that can turn into a monster. You really think you can take Maple so easily?"

"The first step is to get better at expecting the unexpected. Seeing her transform like that definitely threw me."

Pain planned to start by figuring out how to deal with her existing skills. This time Maple had emerged victorious, but who knew what the future might bring. And if nothing else, Pain definitely had the power to go toe to toe with her.

----

780 Name: Anonymous Great Shielder
Yo

781 Name: Anonymous Spear Master
Saw the vid.

782 Name: Anonymous Archer

We've been calling her the walking fortress and the defensive beast but now she's a running fortress and literally a beast.
What are you even supposed to *do?*

783 Name: Anonymous Greatsworder
Just the other day she was human, too.
Whatever she was on the inside.

784 Name: Anonymous Great Shielder
Take your eyes off her one second...and she grows like crazy.

785 Name: Anonymous Mage
How do you grow into artillery guns and full-body replacement?
Explain, please.

786 Name: Anonymous Great Shielder
Legit bolt from the blue stuff.
She goes off on her own for the day and bam, comes back *extra.*

787 Name: Anonymous Spear Master
Only extra? Not ultra? Lolll.

788 Name: Anonymous Greatsworder
Definitely hitting spontaneous mutation levels. Uncanny!

789 Name: Anonymous Archer
But nobody in Maple Tree is normal.
When I saw you in action, I knew.

790 Name: Anonymous Great Shielder
Yeah?

791 Name: Anonymous Archer
Yup.
You were only pretending to be human, Chrome.

792 Name: Anonymous Greatsworder
Maple's so nuts you look regular by comparison, but...
Still, even with that in mind, Sally and the twins are 100% on the side
of cray.

793 Name: Anonymous Mage
I got run over by y'all once.
Just found myself flying through the night air, no warning.

794 Name: Anonymous Archer
A front line that throws metal balls
That's Maple DNA
Clearly not quick on their feet tho

795 Name: Anonymous Spear Master
Right.
They aren't as bad as her, though.

796 Name: Anonymous Great Shielder
They're what happens when Professor Maple gives kids pointers.
She got them there in *one day*.

797 Name: Anonymous Greatsworder
Whaa-?
Is Mapleness catching?

798 Name: Anonymous Mage

Clearly!
Chrome's infected.

799 Name: Anonymous Spear Master
Judging by that vid, absolutely.
Kasumi's the only one who hasn't changed up her gear.
Your back line's pretty wild, too.

800 Name: Anonymous Greatsworder
But you'd still stand a chance one-on-one.
It's the others who are really scary.

801 Name: Anonymous Great Shielder
For real, is there *anyone* who could take Sally head-on?
I went up against her in the guild training room, but that was *not*
happening.

802 Name: Anonymous Archer
Is she *just* dodging?
The vids make it look like she's got more going on.

803 Name: Anonymous Great Shielder
There's rumors, but I think they're just rumors?
Nobody can hit her. That's all.

804 Name: Anonymous Greatsworder
Speaking of Maple Tree rumors...or talk.
That's all you hear out there. The event highlight reel hit everyone
too hard.

805 Name: Anonymous Spear Master

People are calling day three "Armageddon" or "the Apocalypse."

806 Name: Anonymous Great Shielder
'Cause of the clones?
No way to do that solo!

807 Name: Anonymous Archer
Not much difference between no hope and a faint hope.

808 Name: Anonymous Mage
When Pain actually hurt Maple, I was relieved the concept of HP
applies to her.

809 Name: Anonymous Spear Master
But how'd she get that?
Why's she have a last stand skill?
Someone actually hurt her before?

810 Name: Anonymous Great Shielder
Sure.
Not just one, either.
But with her current VIT, probably not happening again.

811 Name: Anonymous Archer
It went up again?
Wasn't it already more than she could ever need?

812 Name: Anonymous Great Shielder
She said she's almost at five digits.
I regretted asking.
Almost fainted on the spot.

813 Name: Anonymous Greatsworder
that's like 100 times my STR
why

814 Name: Anonymous Mage
You get to that point and I can see why you might not want to ever
raise anything else.

815 Name: Anonymous Archer
As long as she's having fun!
Honestly if she raised other stats, who the hell would be able to
handle it?
Like, just running at regular speeds would be a massive power-up.

816 Name: Anonymous Great Shielder
I can't tell if she's spared a thought to efficiency or not.

817 Name: Anonymous Mage
I'd wager she's that strong because she's not thinking at all

818 Name: Anonymous Spear Master
Normal thoughts wouldn't lead to the furball parade float

819 Name: Anonymous Archer
The one image from post-day four

820 Name: Anonymous Greatsworder
The hard cut from Empire's battling to that just blew my mind

----

Defense Build and Post-Event

A few days after the fourth event, the third stratum town was still abuzz with talk of Maple. The subject of rumor was busy relaxing in her guild home.

"Sounds like the fourth stratum is getting added soon. We'll have to go clear the boss together!"

She closed the message from the admins and allowed her imagination to wander, speculating on what the new stratum would be like.

"Hmm…oh! That reminds me."

Maple jumped up from the couch.

"I'd better take care of it before we go any higher. They're expensive, but…"

And with that, she left home, heading across town. Her feet carried her to the shop that sold flying machines.

"I don't *need* one, but…I do wanna have a go! My machines are better, of course. They totally are!"

She emphasized that, like she was trying to mollify the First Machine God. Then she looked over the flying devices in stock.

"Hmm, car-types and machines for four sure do cost a lot.

Maybe I should get a single-seater…but one that's easy to fly. Hngg…"

While she was having analysis paralysis, a voice called her name.

"Maple!"

"Hello."

"Oh, Mai and Yui! Hey, good timing. Which machines are you two using?"

The twins pulled theirs out of their inventories. They'd bought the same flying machines—ones shaped like boots a size larger than their actual shoes.

"Uh, we just use these to fly. It feels like we're levitating!"

Mai demonstrated how to attach them, and once they were on, she floated up off the ground.

"Oh! Wow. But that looks *hard*."

"It is. Yui liked these, so we chose them, but…we've fallen a *lot*."

"I'm so sorry, Mai. I thought it would be easier."

But choosing these did come with certain benefits—

—for one thing, they left both hands free. If monsters attacked in midair, it was easy to fight back.

"Aha… Hmm, I just don't know. Maybe I should get the same kind. Um, is this a good time? Could you show me how to use it?"

"Of course!"

"We'd be glad to."

Maple quickly bought a pair of boot machines. And she started walking toward the field.

"Potentially crashing in town sounds dangerous… Do you know a place without many people?"

"If we head out to the east…"

"Also, Maple, do you mind if we take out some monsters on the way? Grinding is safer when you're with us."

"Oh, sure! Consider yourselves under my protection!" Maple nodded, seeing this as a great way to thank them for teaching her to fly.

It wasn't often she actually walked around the fields these days.

The first thing she did was activate Martyr's Devotion. With that on, the twins were safe as safe could be.

This had proven endlessly useful in the fourth event. A formation that allowed them to cover each other's weaknesses.

"Let's move out!"

""Aye-aye!""

They headed east across the third stratum. This map was designed to make flying everywhere seem easier. There were a lot more monsters on ground level—and stronger ones.

But that wasn't a problem for this team.

""Double Impact!""

Approaching Mai and Yui was like walking right up to death's door. No monsters here could breach Maple's defense; all they could do was shatter and give way.

"You two are so much better at fighting now!"

"Are we...?"

"Mm, maybe? I think so anyway!"

"Maybe we got the hang of it during the event!" Yui said happily. She gave her hammer an extra-strong swing.

"Hmm... I've gotta try harder, too. Maybe I can get better at using my shield! Like...this! Or this!"

Maple started snapping her shield around, miming blocks and parries. The twins saw this and got excited, too, waving their hammers around. They were raising different stats, but Maple's extreme build had taken her to dizzying heights, and she was their original inspiration.

"I hope we can keep getting better... Oh, Mai, incoming!"

"Mm, I see them."

Mai swung her hammer sideways like a bat, sending the approaching monster flying helplessly into the distance.

"As long as we hit, everything goes down after one shot!"

"Yes, and after training with Sally, we hit a lot more often!"

"But she still dodges everything..."

"Hmm, I've never fought the real one, but I've seen her fight a lot, and I honestly don't think I could ever hit her."

Visions of Sally fighting danced before Maple's eyes. She couldn't picture her attacks ever connecting even in her imagination.

After blowing away several more monsters, they reached their destination at last. It was a wide-open field, with ankle-deep grass swaying in the breeze.

"There aren't many monsters here. This is where Chrome took us to practice. So, uh...let's get started!"

Mai and Yui put their machines on again, and Maple followed their lead.

Seeing her feet get much bigger, Maple said, "Oh, it feels just like using Machine God!"

"Boot-types are operated like you're flexing your feet. If you flex too hard, you'll go rocketing away, so..."

Mai demonstrated the gentle approach, floating slowly upward. Then she began flying freely all around, like she had wings.

"Okay, so I flex...yiiiikes!"

When Maple tried, she instantly felt the g-forces...and then her feet went over her head, and she hit the ground face-first.

A loud, resounding clang echoed. Maple was sprawled out on the ground.

"Th-that caught me by surprise…"

"Maple, not that hard! Gently!" Yui said, hovering herself. She was far less stable than Mai, though. Even as Maple watched, she spun into a free fall.

Since she was within range of Martyr's Devotion, she took no damage, but Yui clearly needed a lot more practice as well.

"Yui, how are you still so bad?!"

"I-I'm not! *Sigh…* Okay, stay calm. Stay calm."

This time Yui lifted off into a successful hover.

"*Whew…I did it!*"

Her blunder must have been the result of nerves because Maple was watching. When she flew carefully, Yui was plenty stable.

"Wow… Hmm, flying with Machine God is much easier than this."

"We don't really get how you do that at all," Yui said.

Mai nodded.

"I just go *boom*, and I'm flying. All I gotta do is adjust the direction. I wonder if I can make this work like that?"

Once again Maple tried a big flex but once again instantly lost her balance and wound up with her head buried in the dirt.

This time she didn't get up.

"A-are you okay?"

"It looked like it hurt…but probably didn't…"

"Hngg…"

Maple brushed the dirt off her face and pushed herself upright.

"Everyone else makes it look easy! They're so good."

"Maybe a different machine would help? The back-mounted ones are supposed to be easiest."

"Hngg, it feels a little early to give up just yet. Lemme try a few more times, then I'll think about it."

Maple went back to practicing.

She wasn't *that* slow on the uptake, so she was steadily getting more air time between each crash. Every now and then, monsters attacked, and the twins annihilated them while she kept practicing.

Still, it took the better part of an hour before she could manage a gentle hover.

"O-ohhh! That's more like it!"

She had both hands held out, balancing herself, but was managing to keep herself still for the first time.

"Okay, next, let me try walking—"

Maple moved her feet like a skater, carefully floating forward.

She was definitely moving, but this just didn't feel intuitive at all.

"I just…want to *fly!*"

She flexed her feet hard. She shot forward, but thanks to being able to balance better now, she was soon running across the sky.

"Oh, um… H-how do I stop?!"

Maple knew perfectly well just stopping cold would lead to another fall, so she kept going—and wound up rocketing off into the woods beyond.

"Maple?!"

"A-after her, Yui!"

They gave chase. Somewhere ahead of them, they saw Maple crash into the forest. They flew across the trees, searching the sea of green. Eventually they found a black lump buried headfirst in a tree.

"That you, Maple? You alive?"

"I'm fine! Ugh. I should have taken it slow…"

The twins pulled her out of the tree.

They rose slowly upward, and she summoned Syrup, making it giant.

"Hokay. Yes, this is *much* more relaxing."

Maple settled down on her turtle's back, took off the machine shoes, and stroked her pet's shell.

The twins had shown her the basics, so Maple told herself she could practice more anytime.

"Why don't we focus on getting you two some levels? This flying thing seems like it could take a while."

The twins readily agreed to a change of plans, so Maple had Syrup flew deeper into the woods. Then she had Machine God's armaments lay down suppressing fire as if to prove which machine was better.

◆□◆□◆□◆□◆

While Maple was starting flight practice, Sally was grinding on the third stratum surface.

"*Whew...all right. Hah. So many monsters.*"

She picked up the dropped materials, then glanced down at the machines on her feet.

"I tried several types, but these are just the absolute best."

Sally's inventory had several flying machines in it. But the boot-type offered the most mobility and was perfect for her play style.

When monsters attacked, she could dodge with a quick sideways thrust and then accelerate in a strike.

Sally flew like she was born with wings on her feet.

"Wish we could have used these in the event! Hmm, future stratums are gonna feel slow by comparison."

The machines gave her the ability to move freely in all directions, and she'd incorporated that into her fighting style. This made her much more powerful than when she was stuck on the ground.

"Now I'm hungry for more mobility! There's gotta be some good skills out there that can replicate this!"

But she'd done her research and was well aware there were no leads. If any skills like that were public knowledge, she would've had them already.

"Gotta pin my hopes on more event medals. They might have changed up the list of skills we can redeem those for."

Sally hunted for a while longer, then spotted four familiar players in the distance. Kasumi and Chrome, with Drag and Frederica.

"Erp...she's moving like nobody should again..."

Frederica had seen enough of that in the fourth event—and in their duel before that.

"...Interesting party lineup."

"Yeah...Maple and the twins were out, so...two pairs with nothing better to do."

"And we'll end up fighting again someday. Can't hurt to grab some intel on you guys."

"Not even trying to hide it?" Sally asked.

Drag just grinned back at her. Frederica was hiding behind him, glaring at Sally.

"I'll come duel you again if I find time," she said, scowling. "I wasn't going all out last time, and I feel like I could have done better in the event, too."

Sally readily agreed, then turned to Kasumi.

"Grinding together?"

"More or less. Care to join us? We're headed somewhere with a high spawn rate, so the more the merrier."

Sally didn't have any other plans, so she didn't need much convincing.

The five of them reached a zone at the edge of the third stratum, one filled with much stronger monsters than the area around town.

"Okay, let's start. Taunt!"

Chrome's skill drew the attention of some sturdy-looking iron golems.

"Power Boost! That enough buff for everyone?"

Frederica's spell provided an STR buff, and Kasumi shot forward.

"First Blade: Heat Haze!"

She vanished mid-stride, and an instant later, her blade struck the golem.

"Don't forget about me!" Drag leaped forward like defense was no obstacle, using his giant ax to knock golems around and make the ground itself shudder.

"Quit making me defend you all the time! Multi-Barrier!"

"Covering. Cover!"

Frederica and Chrome were protecting Drag and Kasumi, respectively. Together they made quick work of the advancing golems. Nothing these creatures threw out could ever hit Sally, so nobody worried about protecting her.

"These things are way too slow. No probl— Hmm? Heads up! Up above!"

Sally spotted some mechanical bird monsters swooping toward them and launched herself upward to take them on, her body spinning through the air like an acrobat, dodging and striking down one after the other.

"Mm, definitely in the zone today."

The sky filled with the blue glow of Sword Dance and the red sparks of the damage she dealt.

When she'd cleared the skies and looked down, she saw Drag splitting the last golem's head.

"Ha, not even a challenge!"

"Because I kept you out of harm's way!"

"Yep, thanks! Huge assist."

"It's what I do."

While the Order members were talking, Sally came in for a landing.

"Third stratum monsters just aren't a threat, huh?"

"Not for our guild... Maybe the twins. They don't have the levels yet. And Iz is an exception..."

"Our levels are getting more on par for the upcoming fourth stratum release. Still, no harm in being ready."

The five of them kept moving, searching for more foes—and more XP.

This was a party that spelled certain doom to any monsters that came their way. It was a constant that remained true anywhere either Maple or Sally happened to be.

If the monsters' behavior patterns had included a flight instinct, they would've turned tail just at the sight of them. That's how much stronger these two parties were.

Sally's group disbanded after another two hours of grinding. With nothing else on her plate, Sally headed back to town, and before long, she found herself at the door of their guild home.

"Oh, Sally! You're back!" Maple exclaimed, waving over her menu screen.

"Your group wrap up, too?" Sally asked, sitting down next to her and stretching. "We were out leveling. *Yawn*...I'm pretty worn out."

"Me too! I was fighting for ages. With the twins."

She happily started babbling about their adventures.

"Oh, you grabbed the boot-type, too? They're great! So easy to move in."

"Easy? It was all I could do to float. Maaaaybe fly in one direction. I just keep crashing!"

"It does take a bit of practice." Then Sally shot her a boastful grin. "Heh-heh… Unless you're me, of course. I never crashed once!"

"Arrrrgh! Good for you. Can't say I'm surprised…"

"I mean, if I fell from any height, I'd die, so…that meant I had to be real careful."

"But it's so hard!"

"Oh, we were out with a couple of people from the Order today. I kept a close eye on how they fight. Our guild doesn't have anyone like either of 'em."

Sally launched into a fuller explanation.

"Interesting! But Mai and Yui can bring the pain just as much as Drag can!"

"Yeah, those girls are…something else. Real cheeky. You can't really find anyone like them."

If anyone else played like the twins, Sally would have heard about it.

Everyone would have been gossiping, without a doubt.

"They'll have a lot of attention on them in the next event, and a lot more people will be prepared to face them specifically. We gotta get 'em ready!"

"Absolutely! But we don't know what the next event'll be yet. I hope it doesn't involve racing around the map again…"

Now that she had Atrocity, Maple could cover a lot of ground in a decent amount of time, but she still thought of it as a formidable challenge.

"If it's one of those, you can just work it till you hit whatever personal target you're after. I'll handle the grind to the guild reward."

"Oh? Well, I'll do what I can!"

"Heh-heh. Just don't push yourself too hard. We're not really set up for events that favor crowds."

Even with the twins on board, Maple Tree had only eight

members. Each of them was a powerhouse, but there were definitely times when sheer numbers had the clear advantage.

"Should we find more people?"

"No, not unless you find someone you think you really want. I think we're better off playing it our way, you know?"

Maple clearly agreed with that sentiment.

"Oh, earlier I was thinking about the fourth stratum. I realized I really miss just wandering around town with you."

"Same here! I'm getting sick of grinding levels. Sounds like a good change of pace to me."

"I know, right? Like you said, you can only spend so much time fighting."

Maple's smile proved infectious. Sally considered the idea a moment, then offered a suggestion.

"Why don't we scope out the third stratum town, then? Sounds like you were making a point of getting some flying practice in because you think the fourth stratum isn't far off, right?"

"Mm, yeah! Basically."

"Then let's hit the town as a way of wrapping up our time here. I mean, with all the event prep, we didn't really do much on this stratum."

"Oooh, I'm in! Let's do that!"

Between one event and the other, recruiting members and building them up—they'd been so busy the two of them hadn't really explored the third stratum at all. Which meant there was still loads of fun to be had.

"Unless you're too worn out, Sally?"

"Talking to you gave me a second wind."

"Then let's go have fun!"

"Don't have to tell me twice!"

They jumped up and raced out the door.

"Where to first?"

"Good question. Lots of material shops around here...and equipment."

Even though she suggested it, Sally didn't have a clear goal in mind.

"No need to plan ahead! We'll figure it out as we go. That's usually how I do things anyway!"

"That's why you always come back with stuff that scares the crap out of everyone. But fine by me! Let's do it the Maple way."

"Cool. Then...let's head right! I think I saw a cute shop in that direction once. I don't remember what it sold, though!"

"That *does* sound familiar. Let's check it out!"

"Then follow me!"

Maple took Sally's hand and pulled her along. They were off the beaten path to begin with, and few players came this way, so it was easy to stay together.

It didn't take long before they found the quaint shop Maple had mentioned.

Maple stopped in front, certain this was the place.

"It sells cosmetics? Is that different from accessories?"

Maple took a closer look through the front window.

"Apparently," Sally said. "I'm guessing these just change how you look. Hairstyle or hair color—things like that."

She was already headed in, so Maple trudged after her.

"Excuse us... Oh, you're right. There's so many!"

The shop did sell necklaces and bracelets, ribbons, chokers, and outfits—and like Sally said, hairstyles.

"Well? See anything you want to try?"

"Um, I've got skills that change my hair color...but I wouldn't mind trying a different hairstyle!"

"I'll try something out, myself. How about this one, Maple?"

Sally handed her an item that made hair longer.

And when they added an outfit, Maple looked like an all-new girl.

She was in a long skirt with frills and a white blouse. Paired with the long black hair now flowing down her back, she seemed like a classic beauty.

"W-wow…I don't even recognize myself!"

Maple's hair reached all the way down to her hips. She brought her hand up to it and brushed the fringe, then did a little twirl, which made the skirt's frills billow out, too.

"People who know you would probably figure it out, up close. But damn, it really is a dramatic change!"

"You've gotta try it, Sally! How about these clothes? They're like something the twins would wear!"

"Uh…n-nah, I wouldn't look good in those."

Sally tried to refuse, but that only made Maple's eyes gleam. She stepped closer.

"Heh-heh-heh… It won't hurt to *try*."

Maple had worn what she'd suggested, so Sally couldn't very well refuse. She ended up dressing up in everything Maple wanted.

"Braids…no, pigtails! I've never seen you wear those! Well?"

"Urgh… Th-this is actually excruciating…"

Sally tugged the poofy sleeves of the outfit, refusing to make eye contact.

"Oh?"

But somehow they both ended up buying the new looks.

"I'm gonna put mine on right away!"

"M-maybe someday…I guess…"

Sally gave the new Maple a long look but made no move to change herself. She quickly turned and walked away.

"Ah! Come back here, Sally! Don't you run!"

Maple gave chase and soon caught up, mostly because Sally let her. Then they headed off to explore some more.

This would be their final tour of town—because the fourth stratum was coming soon.

AFTERWORD

First, a big thanks to everyone who's been with me so far. And if this is the first volume you've picked up, I hope you're interested in reading more.

Hi—my name is Yuumikan.

Thanks to your support, *I Don't Want to Get Hurt, so I'll Max Out My Defense* has reached four volumes.

And the manga adaption has started, so I guess it's smooth sailing? I'm grateful either way.

In addition to the bonus story, I made a lot of corrections to this volume's content, making it easier to read and generally more enjoyable.

I think this every time, but I hope the results speak for themselves. Everything around me is changing at dizzying speeds, and I'm doing my best to adjust.

But all these changes are good things, and I'm having a great time.

How is *Bofuri* at four volumes already? Time really flies. Perhaps that's because I'm having such a good time.

I try to remember where I came from—or at least, how much I owe everyone for giving me this opportunity.

A lot of characters appear in this volume, and I hope I managed to communicate their appeal properly.

Now that we've taken a brief look back to where I started and Volume 4 of *I Don't Want to Get Hurt, so I'll Max Out My Defense,* it's about time for us to wrap up.

I promise to keep bringing you the best I can deliver.
I hope you'll stick around for more.
May we meet again someday in Volume 5!

Yuumikan